Transcending Dawn

Vampire Series

Volume One ~ The Deception

Volume Two ~ Shadows of Jealousy

By

P. A. Whitfield

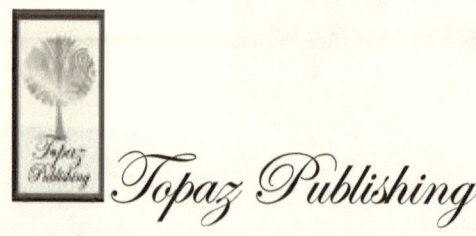

READING ENTERTAINMENT FOR THE ENTIRE FAMILY

Copyright© February 2011, Journey Into Daylight, P.A. Whitfield

Cover Art: Dawne Dominque Copyright September 2013

Editor: Kase J. Reed

Line Editor: Ariana Alexander, Topaz Publishing

ISBN: TPEB000000027 (E-Book)

ISBN-13: 978-0615884028 (Topaz Publishing)

ISBN-10: 0615884024

WC: 61,667

Novella: Topaz Holiday

Genre: Vampire, Paranormal, Sweet Romance

Topaz Publishing, LLC

USA

www.topazpublishingllc.com

DEDICATION

This novel is dedicated to my dear and loving husband, LaVaughn. As I penned this book, he encouraged me every step of the way, even during the late nights when I was tucked away in my office. Your support means more to me than you will ever know. I love you.

Topaz Publishing, LLC

Transcending Dawn~Vampire Series

Volumes One & Two

Feisty and hot tempered, the beautiful Christina Garrett has never experienced true love. At the tender age of eighteen, her father initiated her into the vampire world. *Transcending Dawn* revolves around the relationship between Christina Garrett, a young biracial vampire, and Dylan Duncan, a drachmon warrior. Set in Texas, this paranormal romance is filled with action, suspense, and lighthearted humor.

Chrissie, encumbered by her strict moral upbringing, finds herself enamored by the charming and charismatic Dylan Duncan. Growing up without a father, and the death of her mother, has left her emotionally scarred. Only Dylan, half-human and half dragon, successfully penetrates the protective barriers she has constructed. Although they immediately forge a powerful bond, outside forces conspire to destroy their relationship before it begins.

P. A. Whitfield, Interracial, Sweet, & Paranormal

Romance pawhitfield@earthlink.net
http://www.Topazpublishingllc.com

Thank you for buying a product of Topaz Publishing

Quality Reading for the Entire Family

CONTENTS

VOLUME ONE ~ THE DECEPTION

ACKNOWLEDGMENTS

My Children

Lavaughn, Jr. & Loujuna

Thanks for your support.

Penny Sullivan and Edward Luster

Special Thanks

L. J. Maxie

CHAPTER ONE

The Deception

"The spring semester will begin in a few days. I'll need to select my college classes. Guess Dad is trying to give me a hint by tossing this catalog for East Texas University on my bed. Twenty-five, and he still treats me like a child." Chrissie sauntered over to the bed and plopped down. Though she resented her father's intrusion into her affairs, she unzipped her hoodie, picked up the book and thumbed through it. *"He's coming up the stairs now. I'd know the sound of his footsteps anywhere."*

"Chrissie!" her dad called, as he rapped on her door.

Chrissie glanced up from the booklet and focused on the door. "Yeah, Dad. What is it?"

"May I come in?"

"Sure." She tossed the book aside.

With a sheepish expression on his face, her dad opened the door and ambled into the cluttered bedroom.

"What's up William?"

He chuckled. "William. What brought that on?"

"Just kidding, Dad."

William's smile faded. "Haven't you unpacked yet? This room is still a mess. We've been here a week, already."

Chrissie pushed her hair behind her ear. "Dad. It was your idea to move here in the first place."

"We only moved here because of my job at the university, Peanut." He leaned against the doorframe with arms folded. "Plus, you needed a new start."

"Dad," she warned, "I was doing just fine."

"Enough about moving." He stroked the reddish blonde mustache that draped his crimson lips. "Could I get you to do a favor for me?"

"Depends on what it is." She leaned against her headboard. "You know what they say, '*Don't buy a pig in a poke*'."

"It isn't hard."

Alarms echoed in her brain. "Okay, if it isn't hard, what is it?"

William cleared his throat. "I'm thinking about purchasing the Shack. You know—the campus hangout."

"Ok, and…"

"My lawyer has already drawn up the papers. All I need to do is sign the contracts."

Chrissie raised her palms in question. "And."

William strolled over and sat next to his daughter. "And, I want to buy it for you."

She leaned her head to one side. "Buy it for me. Why?"

"Because you need a separate income."

Smiling, Chrissie nodded. "Okay." She rather liked the idea of independence.

"Oh." William stood. "There's one other thing."

Chrissie drew back to glare at him. "What is it?"

"I was wondering if you would take a drive over there and look around. I want your opinion as a young adult about whether or not you think it's worth the investment. After all, it will belong to you."

She twisted her reddish-blonde spiral between her fingers. "Daddy. I don't know anything about investing."

"Maybe not, but you know what young people like; and your opinion would be invaluable to me."

"I don't want to go," she moaned. "I don't know any of those people." A wide grin spread across her dad's face, but she frowned. "What? Why are you looking at me like that?"

"You looked so much like your mother. You have the same huge almond-shaped eyes she'd flash at me when she wanted something."

"Dad. Are you trying to con me?"

"No." William reached for the picture of Chrissie's mother she kept on the nightstand. Victoria, a gorgeous caramel complexioned woman, had warm brown eyes and thick wavy hair. Even in a photograph, her grace shined through. "You really do resemble your mother." He seemed to float away as he expounded. "The way your ringlets fall into your face — the way you wriggle your nose when you're frustrated; even your slender frame. Everything about you reminds me of your mom."

"Really." Chrissie glanced across the room at her reflection in the mirror. "Did I get this pale complexion or these hazel eyes from my mother?"

William batted his deep-set eyes playfully. "My peepers are *green*, Sweetheart."

"What about this hair?"

"Granted." He grinned in satisfaction. "You do have several of my features."

Chrissie laughed and leaned against her pillow. "Alright, Daddy, I'll do it."

"Thanks, baby." He turned to leave the room, but as he crossed the threshold, he turned and murmured, "You really do look like your mother."

* * * * *

Chrissie drove her 2010 Corvette into the parking lot of the Shack. The small yellow structure didn't seem worth her father's time. She parked as close to the crowded entrance as possible. Tapping her fingers on the dashboard, she surveyed the large number of college students that loitered in the front of the building.

Her dad had recently secured the position as professor of economics at the local university. A colleague had informed him that the proprietor of the Shack had decided to retire. His innate ability to sense a bargain had been stimulated by the opportunity. As a result, William had enlisted her as his spy to ascertain the amount of activity at the club.

When Chrissie opened the car door, the fragrance of pine filled her nostrils. Huge evergreens swayed overhead in the breeze, giving the building an intimate atmosphere. As she exited the vehicle, she evaluated her surroundings. A sudden gust of January wind pushed against her slender frame. After pulling her jacket together, she walked toward the front entrance. The first snowflakes of winter dusted her lashes, melted, and ran down her cheek. She heard the summer had been exceptionally hot. Hopefully, the cooler weather was a welcomed change.

The enormity of the building's interior caught her by surprise, and she gasped. Outside, the appearance had misrepresented the actual size of the structure. In awe, she marveled at the soft blue walls, which were decorated with posters of popular music stars. You name the genre, and it was represented on the walls of the Shack.

The cozy décor astonished her as well. Two rows of scarlet booths with a narrow aisle between them lined the walls. An ornate wooden railing separated the seating from the dance floor, which served as the focal point of the room. On the ceiling, three mammoth fans were suspended from wooden rafters on both sides of the room.

Couples sat in booths and made out unabashedly to the romantic melody emanating from an antique jukebox at the back of the room. Other couples caressed on the dance floor, seeming to luxuriate in the joy of touching and being touched. From a separate room near the kitchen, Chrissie could hear the whack of a pool cue as it smashed against a billiard ball. Like most vampires, her hearing was acute. She also detected the sound of cards being shuffled in another room.

Chrissie twitched her nose as the pungent odor of onions and cooking beef floated from the kitchen. All in all, the establishment buzzed with the activities of youth. Yes, the business had potential; she would recommend the purchase to her dad.

Chrissie scanned the room for an empty seat, but to her chagrin, the one available booth was in the back near the kitchen. All those wondering eyes would focus on her as she made her way through the crowd. With the booth in view, Chrissie steeled herself and trudged down the constricted pathway toward the rear of the building. As she passed various tables, she heard couples discussing whether anyone recognized her from school. Being the topic of interest embarrassed her; she winced at the unwanted attention.

Traversing the sea of faces seemed to take an eternity. At last, Chrissie scooted into her booth, and then absorbed the ambiance around her. Rhythmic music captivated her senses, and she focused on the dance floor.

A slender young woman with short blonde hair carried a pen and pad. She strolled over to Chrissie's table. "What can I get for you tonight?"

Chrissie lifted her head and took in her name tag. "Hi, Jena. Do you serve herbal tea?"

"Sure." She beamed. "Will there be anything else?"

"No, nothing else, thank you." When the server flitted away, Chrissie refocused on the dance floor. All the couples, except one, seemed lost in each other. A young man stood about six-three and the woman he was dancing with was about five-seven. Each time the woman attempted to cuddle, the guy would step back, keeping her body at a distance. This entire scenario seemed odd. In most instances, it was the female who avoided physical contact. Their interaction was interesting—different from the others. Chrissie couldn't resist eavesdropping on their conversation.

The young woman scowled and stood up straight. "What is your problem tonight, Dylan?"

Narrowing his eyes, Dylan retorted, "Nothing."

She flinched, then gazed around the room. "Why don't we go somewhere, so we can be alone?"

Dylan sighed. "Kaylee, this is just a dance, nothing more. We dated for a while, but it didn't work out. Let's just leave it alone, okay?"

"I've missed you," the woman pressed, "so much. Don't you miss our relationship at all?"

The guy rolled his eyes. "What relationship?" he snapped. "I just told you—we never had a relationship. There was a physical attraction. Nothing more. It's over."

"How can you say that?" she whined, her eyes clouded.

Dylan didn't respond. Instead, he maintained his distance. Chrissie wondered how this young woman could stand the humiliation. When the song ended, Dylan twirled on his heels and sauntered away. Kaylee stormed back to the booth she shared with three other young females.

With the entertainment at an end, Chrissie turned to gaze out of the window. She found herself enthralled by the accumulation of snow.

The waitress returned with her order, breaking her thoughts. "It's snowing, huh? Well, in East Texas, the best you can hope for is slush."

Relaxed over her cup of herbal tea, Chrissie's mind drifted back to events of the past few days. Moving into a new house, her first days at college, and her dad's new position occupied her mind. Though her life hummed with activity, Chrissie felt lost and alone. To add insult to injury, everyone around her knew each other and intermingled with ease. Their camaraderie reinforced her feelings of isolation.

"Hello," a male's voice echoed above her.

Chrissie shifted her eyes from the frost-covered window to espy the young man called Dylan, towering above her.

Appearing to wait for her answer, he stood with his hands behind his back. His long dark lashes created the perfect complement for his rich brown eyes. Dark brown bangs draped his naturally tan face and swept across the middle of his forehead. A smile played across his lips. "Hi, my name is Dylan — Dylan Duncan. Do you mind if I sit with you?" He glanced around the room. "This place is crowded, tonight. There isn't another empty seat."

Trying not to stare, Chrissie swallowed the lump in her throat. "S, sure," she stammered.

Dylan peeled off his black leather jacket, exposing his broad chest. Huge biceps bulged beneath his fitted green shirt. He plopped down in the seat across from her, tossed his jacket over the back of the booth, and then flashed a gorgeous smile.

Chrissie remained still, not wanting to call attention to herself. Dylan leaned forward and raised her chin. "Hey. Are you ok? You seem a little nervous."

"I'm fine." She turned from his prying eyes.

He pointed to the table. "Were you holding this seat for someone?"

To avoid making eye contact, Chrissie peered at her cup of tea. She mumbled, "No."

Appearing relaxed, Dylan spread his arms over the length of the booth. "You look to be about—what? Eighteen or so. Are you a freshman?"

Chrissie brightened. "I *am* a freshman. But..." For a second, she pondered. Her father had warned her not to reveal her real age, but the truth poured out. "I'm twenty-five."

"Whoa. Twenty-five." He scratched the back of his neck. "You're a little old for a freshman, aren't you?"

Miffed, Chrissie darted her eyes from side to side. "Ah, ah, dad and I traveled a lot," she lied. "You know the old saying, better late than never."

He grinned. "Yeah. I've got a year left myself. Graduation will be sweet."

At that point, Jena strolled over to the table. "What will it be, Dylan?"

For a moment, Dylan scanned the menu board over the counter. "Um, give me the usual; a double cheeseburger, rare, a frappe, and a large fry. Oh, snatch the meat off the cow and throw it on the bun. Last time, it was over cooked." At that, Dylan glanced at Chrissie. "Would you like anything to eat? I mean. Tea. Really? Who goes out, just to drink tea?"

Chrissie shook her head. "No, thank you."

"I guess that's it." While Jena bounced away, Dylan glanced over his shoulder. Turning back to Chrissie, he held a rather puzzled expression but grinned. "What classes are you taking this year?"

"The basics," she replied quietly.

A serious look crept across his face. "May I ask you something?"

Caressing the warm cup in her hand, Chrissie shrugged. "I guess."

Dylan smiled, placed his elbow on the table, and allowed his chin to rest in his palm. "Do you always give such short answers?"

A broad grin swept across her face, and she chuckled. "I'm sorry. I didn't realize I was giving you short answers."

"Now, that's more like it. You have a stunning smile. You should show it more often."

Seven years ago she would have blushed at that comment. However, much had changed since that time. Chrissie smiled once more. "Can we start over?"

"We most certainly can." Dylan extended his hand. She reciprocated. "By the way, what is your name?"

She raised her cup to her lips. "My name is Christina, Christina Garrett."

He leaned forward and stared into her face. "Have we met before?" A glimmer of recognition gleamed in his eyes.

Feeling as if he had stolen the line from an old movie, Chrissie answered, "No. I don't think so."

Dylan raised a brow. "I've heard that name somewhere else today—I know I've heard..." He snapped his fingers and pointed at her. "I know where I've heard that name. My new economics professor. His name is Garrett, William Garrett. Are you acquainted with him?"

Chrissie widened her eyes and whispered, "He's my dad."

"Wow. What's it like having a professor for a dad?" Dylan elevated his voice as if astonished by his findings.

"Most people don't think of teachers as normal. For some unknown reason, they think they're manufactured on an assembly line. It's quite the opposite. It's just like having anyone else for a dad." She pressed her lips as if to bite her tongue. "He gets on my nerves sometimes, but I guess all parents annoy their kids."

A woman standing above the table drew Chrissie's attention. Kaylee, had ogled her since Dylan sat down. Now, she pranced toward the couple with arms folded. Tossing her auburn hair off her shoulders, she glared at Chrissie. "The guys are going to catch the nine o'clock movie. Why don't you join us?"

Never glancing upwards, Dylan's face hardened. "I don't think so," he muttered. "I plan to crash pretty early tonight."

Her face ashened; Kaylee placed her hands on her hips. "Well." She turned and sprinted away. Under her breath, she mumbled what sounded like profanity. "Just wait," she grumbled. "You think Dylan won't use you just because you're pretty. He'll throw you over, like he did me." Kaylee's behavior clearly demonstrated she had not relinquished her claim on Dylan.

Her caustic remarks caused Chrissie to flinch. She noticed how Dylan glanced in Kaylee's direction and back again.

"That's alright," Kaylee spewed. "It'll be a matter of time before he dumps you too. Then, I'll be the one laughing. Tramp."

Sometimes, Chrissie wished her ears weren't so keen. Hearing everything people said could get a bit tedious, especially when *she* was the subject of their ire.

Fortunate for Chrissie, Jena returned from the kitchen with Dylan's order. She placed it before him and departed. Chrissie watched the steam rising from the burger. "I guess you two broke up, huh?"

"Nah." Dylan reached for his frappe. "We only dated a few times." He took a sip and frowned. "It didn't work out — too possessive!"

Chrissie peered over her shoulder. Kaylee sat with arms folded. The scowl on her face was evident even in the shadows of the room. "She seems a little bothered by my presence."

He shook his head. "Like I said. She's a possessive flake."

Dylan lifted his rare burger to his mouth. Blood oozed from the sandwich and splattered onto the plate below. He licked his fingers and paused. "Would you like to share my burger? There's plenty."

"No, thank you." Chrissie's mouth watered when she noticed the blood stained plate. She longed to share that burger, but her diet wouldn't permit it. Dylan gobbled down the burger in record time. Wide-eyed, she gawked at his amazing appetite. *"It's a wonder he didn't choke to death."*

"I guess I was pretty hungry," he admitted, as he swallowed the last bite.

"You. Must. Have. Been. Starving." She winced. "I can't ever remember seeing anyone devour a meal so quickly."

"Yeah. I guess I was pretty hungry." He wiped his mouth with the back of his hand. "I haven't had anything to eat since last night. I overslept this morning ...had to meet with my major advisor at eight, so I didn't have time to eat. Enough about me." He rested his chin on his closed fist and scrutinized her face. "You know, you look like your dad."

The truth about her parentage would probably raise brows. Keeping her secret, Chrissie smirked. "People tell me that all the time."

"I know your dad's a professor, but what does your mom do?"

In most cases, she didn't like discussing her personal life, particularly with strangers, but somehow sharing her life with Dylan seemed natural. She shifted her gaze to the wall. "My mom died of brain cancer when I was ten."

With narrowed eyes, Dylan muttered, "Humph. Looks like we have a lot in common. Both of us have one surviving parent. My dad died last year."

Without considering his feelings, she blurted out, "Do you mind if I ask what happened?"

Dylan sighed. "I don't talk about it often, but for some reason, I don't mind sharing it with you."

They shared the same sentiment about divulging personal information. Chrissie found this fascinating.

For a moment, Dylan appeared lost in thought. With bitterness in his voice, he continued. "My dad died during a hunting trip with his best friend — my new stepdad, Marcus Banachek. According to Marcus, my dad collapsed. He was unable to carry his body back by himself. When Marcus led the rescue party back to recover the body, it had mysteriously disappeared." He paused and stared at his hands. "Six months later, he married my mother."

The anger in his eyes spoke volumes. As the strobe lights flashed overhead, Chrissie spotted green specks in his brown eyes. Of that, she was sure. She squinted to get a better look, but the emerald glow had vanished. "*Just the light,*" she told herself. Perhaps, she should change the subject. Curiosity got the better of her, and she pressed for more information. "Did you ever find out what happened?"

"No, I never did. I have my suspicions. The worthless drone! But, it wouldn't hold up in court."

Chrissie felt awful for having broached the subject. Her sharp teeth grazed her bottom lip. "I'm sorry."

At first, he feigned a smile, but then he knitted his brow. "Don't be. Someday, I'll find the truth. Then, there will be hell to pay."

Once again, Chrissie spotted sparks of emerald in his eyes. "Maybe there is nothing to know. It could have happened just as your stepfather said."

"That's the problem." Dylan clinched his fist. "He never explained anything. He just said he died, and because he's a warrior, no one questioned his word." A scowl wrinkled his brow, and he pounded his fist on the table.

The couples seated on either side of them jumped when they heard the thud. No one muttered a word. Clearly, they were aware of Dylan's volatile behavior. The sudden emotional outburst had startled Chrissie, too, but when she observed the sadness in his eyes, she understood his reaction all too well. She rested her elbows atop the table. "Warrior?"

Dylan blinked, bringing him out of his daze. "Huh?" His eyes fluttered again. "Oh, uh. Weekend warrior. You know; hunter, fisherman, all-round sportsman."

"Oh, okay."

Dylan elevated his darkened eyes and stared directly at her. "I never got to say goodbye."

"Trust me," she replied, with caution. "It wouldn't have helped if you had said good-bye. My mother was in the hospital when she passed away. My grandmother and I had the opportunity to say our good-byes, but it didn't change anything." Remembering the hurt she'd felt that day, Chrissie stared into space, unblinking. "I still miss her. It was as if I hadn't had that chance. I still get just as angry about her leaving me."

He crushed a napkin in his hand. "At least you got to say good-bye."

"Yeah," Chrissie nodded. "I guess that's something to be grateful for although I don't feel like it now. Maybe someday I'll feel differently."

"I'm sure you will."

* * * * *

Three hours took flight as the couple sat and talked. By the end of the evening, Chrissie felt as though she'd known Dylan for years. They clicked—talking about everything. The relationship with his stepfather was strained to say the least. On a lighter note, they discussed his many lighthearted adventures on campus.

With empty cups between them, Dylan extended his hand. "Would you like to dance?"

Chrissie grinned. "Sure, why not?"

Before she knew what was happening, Dylan got up, strolled to her side of the table, and helped her out of the booth. He placed his hand at the small of her back and led the way down the steps to the dance floor. Then, he took her in his powerful arms and held her close. Together, they swayed to the rhythm of a slow melody. As they glided across the floor, Chrissie marveled at his grace.

Dylan closed his eyes and inhaled. "You smell wonderful,"

"Why, thank you."

"I've never smelled perfume like this before. What are you wearing?"

Her dad had cautioned her about divulging too much information about herself. The enticing fragrance of vampires' bodies attracted their victims. Although she debated the idea, she saw no harm in the answer. "I'm not wearing a fragrance."

Biting the inside of his jaw, he leaned back to glare at her. "You're not? You mean that's your natural scent."

His reaction surprised her, and she regretted her honesty. "It's probably my soap or my shampoo," she lied.

"Oh, I hadn't thought of that."

She contrived a smile, and they dropped the subject, remaining silent for the rest of the dance. After the song ended, they made their way back to the booth. Again, Dylan placed his hand on her back, but this time, a quivering sensation surged through her body.

Without warning, he grinned and asked, "Do you have a boyfriend?"

Nervous because of his prying question, Chrissie sputtered, "W, what? Why?"

"I'm wondering if some jealous guy will come in here and try to punch me out."

Pressing her lips together, Chrissie glowed. "You don't have to worry about that. I just moved here, and I haven't met many people."

"Good. I didn't want anyone buggin' out. That means I have an open playing field."

Chrissie didn't know whether to believe Dylan or not. She hoped he was sincere, but as he revealed by a spurned Kaylee, he did have a nasty reputation.

Kaylee chose that moment to meander past their table. "I'm leaving now, Dylan," she announced, loud enough for the entire room to hear.

He glanced over his shoulder. "Tell me why I should care," he muttered, turning back to Chrissie.

Chrissie winced as Kaylee leered. Suddenly, she stormed away. "She's furious. You know that, right?"

Dylan waved his hand. "That drone? She's always furious. I told you we stopped seeing each other long ago. She has this fixation with greatness." He leaned toward Chrissie and brushed a curl that framed her face.

Although Dylan had been sharp with Kaylee, his gentle nature drew her to him. "Maybe if you talk to her."

"Maybe I don't want to talk to her. She's a poster child for the nut house."

Chrissie stroked her cheek. "I don't know. Something's going on in her mind." She stuck the tip of her fingernail in her mouth and mused. *"She does seem a little obsessed with him."*

"Chrissie, she's hardly worth my time. She has no mind — only a shell."

Entranced by the deep conversation, Chrissie lost all track of time. For the first time in seven years, she felt a connection to someone other than her father. When she glanced at the clock, she realized it was after 11:00. Dad was probably at home wondering what happened to her, not that her father had a valid reason to worry. She had the ability to care for herself, yet she felt compelled to leave. "I didn't realize it had gotten so late. I need to go. My father is going to be worried about me."

"Yeah," Dylan looked at his watch, "it is getting pretty late. Can I drive you home?"

"Wow." Chrissie was taken aback by his invitation. "No thanks. I have my own car."

Flashing a stunning smile, Dylan leaned in. "Well. At least I can walk you to your car? I mean, you aren't scared of the boogie man, are you?"

Somewhat lightheaded, Chrissie uttered. "Of course not."

They both laughed as Dylan got up and helped her out of the booth. When she stood, he ogled her body from head to foot. His crude methods made her feel awkward. "Are you an athlete?" he asked, never shifting his gaze.

She glanced at the floor. "Yes, I am." It pleased her that he had noticed. "Or rather, I was in high school. Why do you ask?"

"Your body is *very* well-developed for a girl." He seemed amazed that a girl would take care of her physique.

"What do you mean, for a girl?" Dylan reached for her coat, which was draped over the back of the seat. He held it as she slipped her arms into the sleeves. "What are you trying to say?"

Raising both his hands as though he were being arrested, he laughed. "No offense, but most of the girls I've known don't go in for sports. Too sweaty." Chrissie turned to walk away. Dylan grabbed his jacket and threw it on.

"Maybe you've been hanging out with the wrong girls." She smirked.

Dylan didn't reply. "What did you play?"

"Basketball, softball, and volleyball," she boasted. She always took pride in gloating about her physical accomplishments. "If you could throw it, bounce it, or hit it, I played it."

"Wow, you are an athlete."

"What about you? Your body is well-toned, too." She smiled to herself. *"In truth, Michelangelo could not have chiseled a more perfect specimen."*

"Who me? I don't play sports, but I work out a few times a week." He patted his rock hard abs. "Have to keep the old midsection in shape."

They left the Shack and stood in the parking lot. "Do you belong to a gym in town?" Chrissie yearned for an invitation to join him there.

"No, I have a set of weights in my apartment, and I workout at home."

Chrissie lowered her eyes doubtfully. "You must have a great deal of self-discipline. Not many people have the resolve to maintain a regular exercise schedule without some type of extrinsic motivation."

"It's a habit." Dylan's voice brightened. "I've been working out as long as I can remember. My dad started me when I was a little boy, and I guess it's ingrained in me now."

As they stepped into the light, Chrissie heard someone mumbling in the distance. "Had to crash early tonight, yeah right! This isn't over, Dylan. Just wait!" It was Kaylee's voice. Chrissie glanced upwards. Kaylee appeared to be skulking next to an enormous oak tree, bare of leaves from the winter's cold. It didn't surprise Chrissie that she would be lurking in the dark, waiting for Dylan.

Although ostensibly oblivious to Kaylee's presence, Chrissie noticed Dylan's eyes narrow when she made the remark. *"He couldn't have heard a comment spoken so softly. The wind must have stung his eyes."* Suddenly, the sound of twigs snapping in the underbrush caught her attention. Something large moved toward Kaylee. Chrissie elevated her nose and sniffed. The creature prowling in the darkness was canine. *"Just a dog,"* she thought.

Chrissie and Dylan's turned their heads simultaneously as Kaylee bolted from behind the tree, a look of terror on her face. "Run," she screamed, as she raced for her car. When she reached her vehicle, she snatched the door open, jumped inside, and slammed the door behind her. Her engine roared to life, and she sped away.

At first, Chrissie found Kaylee's escapade amusing. She smirked to herself. *"Afraid of a dog."* Then, a huge black and tan Rottweiler staggered from the woods, its bristled fur wet from the new fallen snow. Froth dripped from its snarling mouth.

The couple stood halfway between Chrissie's car and the building with no means of escape. Subduing the animal would have presented no problem for her, but she couldn't allow Dylan to witness her actions. Unable to think of an appropriate response, she let out an ear-piercing screech.

The deranged dog seemed drawn to her cries. His wild eyes locked on her as steam rose from its damp coat. Inside, Chrissie wanted desperately to wring its neck, but instead, she lurched backwards. Her sudden movement triggered an instinctive reaction in the beast. Like lightning, the ailing animal vaulted for her.

As the dog leaped for Chrissie's throat, Dylan swept her behind him. With the back of one hand, he swatted the massive body into the side of a parked car. The canine struggled for a second before it wobbled to its feet. Once again, the crazed canine bolted for her.

This time, Dylan caught the creature in midair. The dog wriggled violently, sinking its froth filled fangs into his arm. Dylan looked at the blood seeping from his torn sleeve, then gnashed his teeth. With one twist of his powerful hands, he cracked the animal's thick neck, and threw it to the ground.

Chrissie sprinted to him. "Are you okay?"

He stood with his back to her. "I'm fine," he answered without turning.

Blood drenched the sleeve of his jacket. Chrissie touched his arm. "You're hurt."

"It's just a scratch." He pulled away.

Chrissie tried to examine his expression, but his eyes were closed. "That dog was rabid." Dylan didn't respond. For a solid minute, he stood stationary; eyes shut. She wondered if she needed to call a doctor, but she stood by his side in silence.

When he finally opened his eyes, he gazed at her. "Let's get you to your car."

"Dylan, I think you should see a doctor."

"I'll go to the ER as soon as we get you to your car." He smiled at her. "Really. I will."

The pair strolled to her car, neither of them speaking. When they reached her vehicle, Dylan stopped and shoved his hands into his pockets. "I really enjoyed talking to you tonight. Would you mind if I call you sometime?"

"Would I mind?" Chrissie was elated but didn't want to appear desperate. She kept her tone as nonchalant as possible. "If you'd like. My number is 404 333-0011."

"Wait a sec. Let me put it in my phone." He took his phone from his pocket and without having her repeat the digits, he entered them. It thrilled her that he remembered the number. She noticed he'd put her on speed dial, and her heart leaped for joy.

"Well, good night, Dylan. Maybe I'll see you around campus."

"Oh, you will most definitely see me — and soon." Dylan pulled his hands from his jeans. Chrissie had left the car door unlocked, so she reached out and opened it. He furrowed his brows. "Do you always leave your car unlocked? That's dangerous you know." Were his concerns genuine?

"I know. My father is always chastising me about that," she lied. In reality, her dad never worried about her safety. She could take down an elephant if she needed to. "Promise. I'll try to remember to lock it next time."

Dylan chuckled. "You'd better. I would hate for anything to happen to you."

His words thrilled Chrissie. She'd never believed in love at first sight, but with Dylan, she almost accepted the possibility. After getting into her car, she drove away, keeping an eye on Dylan in the rearview mirror.

⋆ ⋆ ⋆ ⋆ ⋆

The night was exceedingly dark, typical of a January evening. Chrissie allowed her mind to wander as the trees whizzed by. She visualized the contour of Dylan's face. His powerful squared jaws were set against a thick mass of curly dark brown hair. The luminosity in his eyes was astounding. Broad shoulders accentuated his athletic frame. For a moment, Chrissie allowed herself the pleasure of fantasizing about his lips touching hers — loving and being loved.

But then, a haunting memory disturbed her thoughts. One night, her adoptive dad had broken his silence and revealed the truth about her. Now, her mind rambled back to that night. She recalled standing in her room, packing for the move to Texas.

Her dad sauntered in, a pleasant interruption of an undesirable task. "Sweetheart, I need to talk to you."

"Ok, what's up?" She pushed the clothes to one side of the bed and then sat down.

William bit his lip, inhaled and asked, "Have you noticed that almost everyone comments on how much you look like me?"

"Yeah. I've been told more than a few times that I bear a striking resemblance to you." She laughed lightheartedly. "I guess it's true what they say... if you feed someone long enough, they begin to resemble you."

He strolled to her desk, took a deep breath, and spun to face her. With apprehension in his eyes, he confessed. "Sweetheart, there is something I've neglected to tell you. I don't know how you'll react to this knowledge, but the time has come for you to know the truth."

"What truth?" Her dad's tone alarmed her. Fear of what he might say gripped her heart.

William swallowed hard and with a sigh, he blurted out the truth, "I am your biological father, and not just the monster who sired you."

"What?" In an effort to process his statement, her mind swirled. *"How could he be my biological father? After all, vampires can't father children, or so I thought."* She raised her eyes to meet his. "What do you mean? How is that possible?" she asked, her mind unable to grasp the information.

As if he were searching the depths of her soul, William gazed at her with piercing green eyes. "I met your mother when I was a professor at Sutton University. She was twenty-one at the time, and the most gorgeous young woman I had ever seen. Her smooth caramel skin and dark brown eyes made my heart melt. I tried my best to stay away from her, because I felt any advances toward her would have been ill-advised and morally wrong. You see, I was thirty-nine." He shook his head at the memory. "I knew I should have kept my distance."

Still in a daze, she said, "This doesn't make sense. You're a vampire."

"I hadn't been sired then. I was nothing more than a professor of economics. That fall, her first year as a graduate student, she enrolled in my class. She came to me for tutoring. As brilliant as she was, I knew she didn't need the help, but I enjoyed her company. We spent countless hours together alone in my office. After a time, one thing led to another. Before I realized what was happening, we were embroiled in a passionate love affair."

Rage exploded within Chrissie. All her life she'd wondered about her father. Now, this man, whom she'd idolized as a parent for seven years, was telling her, he'd left her mother pregnant and alone. She sprang to her feet. "Mom died when I was ten years old! Where were you all those years? Did you leave her to fend for herself because a biracial baby wasn't in your plans?" Venom spewed from her in torrents.

"No," he answered, "it wasn't like that at all. I adored your mother. I planned to ask her to marry me. We made arrangements to meet in the park one night after her last class, but she was running late. So, I sat down on a bench to wait for her. Gazing at that dazzling Harvest moon, I felt excited about our rendezvous, and contemplated just how to pop the question."

William closed his eyes. A faint smile crossed his lips, but it quickly morphed into an expression of shear horror. "As I sat reveling in my feelings of love, I thought I heard something, or someone moving behind me. When I turned, someone grabbed my throat and lifted me straight into the air. I couldn't budge. He locked me in an inescapable grip. Struggle as I might, I couldn't break his hold. In a flash, his teeth ripped the flesh from my neck, and I writhed in pain. At that precise moment, a group of students crossed the street. Had it not been for them, I would have been drained. After that encounter, it was all blue Mondays for a while. I drifted in and out of consciousness. I don't remember any details, just the pain.

Chrissie wanted to reach out and comfort him, but the rage continued to burn inside her. She needed to strike out and wound him as he had wounded her. Instead, she rolled her eyes and barked, "So, what happened to you after that?"

William leaned against the desk. His voice was almost imperceptible. "When the pain subsided, I had this insatiable thirst. I'm ashamed to say I attacked the first person I saw. And well, let's just say, he didn't fare too well."

Chrissie balled her fists. The more William talked the angrier she got. Finally, she shook with fury. "What does that have to do with my mother?"

He sighed. "As much as I loved your mother, I knew I could never see her again. How could I put her life in that kind of danger?" William's voice cracked. "I can't seem to find the right words. There's no other way to say this. I was a madman, Chrissie. I retained no self-control, no semblance of my former self. I had no mentor...no one to teach me—to show me how to survive in this new form. It's a miracle no one discovered my secret that first year."

Chrissie understood, perhaps better than anyone else in the world. Even so, she still couldn't contain the anger. "So you chose never to see her again, and never to see me at all. What did it feel like to know you had a child out there, and just walk away?"

After taking a deep breath, William cleared his throat, then continued. "After the fever of the new birth wore off, I searched for Victoria and tracked her down. Much to my chagrin, I discovered she had passed away of cancer. I stayed in Pinole to remain near her grave. Then one day, I spotted this beautiful little girl who looked like Victoria; except she had some of her father's features as well. She had long reddish blonde ringlets. Her soulful hazel eyes could charm a bird from a tree." He gazed into Chrissie's eyes. "That little girl was you. You had my pallor and my hair. But to me, you looked so much like your mother." A hint of a smile crossed his lips.

Deep creases etched her brow. "And then what? You just walked away."

With doleful eyes, William stared at her. His tone remained serene. "No, Peanut. I watched you at a distance for years—at your softball games, at the park, at the movies. I was there the first time your grandmother allowed you to date Jay."

"You were watching when I went out with Jay?"

Drifting away on a cloud of memories, William continued. "You looked so gorgeous with your hair swept up...a regular beauty queen."

William's composure fueled Chrissie's irritation. "If you knew about me, why did you let Nana raise me all those years?"

Her indignation appeared to spark rage in him. "Are you kidding? Have you forgotten what I am? All I could offer you was existence, not life."

Unable to control herself, she yelled. "So what happened to change your mind? How is it that you couldn't bring yourself to change Mom, but you could change me? Was my life not as important as hers?"

True to his character, William regained his poise. "Do you recall the day I met you in the hospital? You were in your bed, wracked with pain."

Riddled with anger, Chrissie tossed her clothes about the bed. "What does this have to do with anything?"

With misery in his eyes, William clutched her arm, which forced her to focus on his face. "Calm down and listen to me. You were dying. The doctors diagnosed you with terminal brain cancer; the same cancer that claimed your mother's life! I wasn't there to prevent Victoria's death, but I sure as hell wasn't going to sit back and watch you die too!"

Annoyed by her father's confession, Chrissie ripped her arm from his grasp and furrowed her brow. "Nana never told me I had terminal cancer. If I had it, why didn't she tell me?"

William shrugged. "I don't know why she didn't tell you. I guess she wanted your last days to be peaceful." He picked up a pair of jeans that had fallen on the floor. "You know my skills. I can smell an illness inside a human. All of their diseases have particular smells."

The truth of William's words pierced her stubbornness, and she calmed herself. "You're right," she admitted, taking the pants from his hands, "but I still don't understand why you changed me."

In a soothing hypnotic voice, William explained, "I had been without you for eighteen years. I wanted—no, I needed my child. Can you understand that, Christina—how much a parent wants to be with his child? I thought if I were to change you, you and I could move through eternity together. Father and daughter. Against the world."

He sat on the bed, and Chrissie scooted beside him. "I was standing across the street the night the ambulance came for you. I didn't know what had occurred, so I trailed you to the hospital. At the first opportunity, I slipped into your room. When I saw how frail—how weak you were, it ripped my heart out. You had so many machines hooked up to you. They had them on your head, your chest," he closed his eyes, "and your arms. You moaned, and I could smell death in the room. Cancer had riddled you frail frame. At that point, I knew you were dying. I called your name, and you opened your eyes, but you couldn't see me." William shook his head and stared at the floor. "The doctors could do nothing more than prolong your death, so I fused my blood with yours. You were already so weak. It didn't take very much to slow your heart rate until it was imperceptible. You had a pulse, but the heart monitor couldn't pick it up. Of course, the monitor sounded when it failed to detect a heartbeat."

The depth of his agony reflected in his eyes. They revealed anguish, generated by years of loneliness. Chrissie felt chinks in her emotional armor. "I remember seeing your face," she grimaced, "and wondering who you were. I don't remember being bitten."

"Have you forgotten what looking into my eyes can do to a human? I realized the trauma you'd endure during the transformation. I made sure the initiation caused you as little pain as possible. However, the nurse entered the room to check on your condition sooner than I had anticipated, so I leaped out your window. According to their instruments, you were gone. She called a code blue and immediately began CPR. When the doctor arrived, he pronounced you dead. As soon as the team left the room, I returned, rescued you, and took you home. I've been afraid to tell you the truth. I didn't know what Victoria's family had told you about me."

Chrissie wrung her hands. "Nana admitted she didn't know anything about you. She didn't know your name, and she had no idea if you knew about me."

William winced. "I didn't. I was transformed before Victoria told me about you. I don't know if she was aware of the pregnancy before I disappeared." Despair dimmed his eyes. He crossed the room, opened the top draw of the desk, and removed a gold framed picture of Chrissie's mother. Transfixed, he ran his fingers over her face and murmured, "She was the love of my life. You are the fruit of that love. You have no idea how much I adored your mother—how much she loved me. How could I allow our love's creation to perish?"

The ice in Chrissie's heart thawed. For the first time, she saw her father as a forlorn, broken individual whose world had been shattered by someone else's bloodlust. He and her mother could have had a wonderful life together. The thought broke her heart. Now, Chrissie felt the depth of his heartache. From that point, they were inseparable. The pain they shared served as an umbilicus joining their lifeless hearts together.

CHAPTER TWO

Concerns

When Chrissie realized where she was, she had pulled into the open garage of her home. After getting out of the car, she meandered to the door. Turning the key in the lock, she then eased it open. As she suspected, her dad was waiting for her. He strolled out of his den. "Did you have any trouble tonight?"

"What kind of trouble would you expect me to have? It isn't as though I can't take care of myself." Chrissie's defenses rose. Her dad would never approve of her friendship with Dylan, and she resented that fact.

A look of guilt distorted William's unnaturally pale countenance. "You know what I mean. It's been almost a month since we consumed human blood. I wondered if you might have succumbed to temptation."

"Lay off, Dad. I didn't slip. I can wait until we get a new supply. There are other sources of blood in Texas." Sarcasm laced her voice. "Isn't that why we moved here — where the deer and the antelope play?"

"I'm sorry, baby, I was just speculating as to why you were so late."

"Why didn't you just ask?" Seeing the hurt in his eyes, Chrissie felt ashamed of herself. "I'm sorry," she relented. "I guess I'm a little edgy."

"If you don't mind my asking, what's wrong?" As it is with all fathers, William's concern was obvious.

Chrissie threw her keys on the coffee table and plopped on the loveseat. "I don't want to talk about it."

"It might help." He eased down on the sofa next to her.

Her dad was right. It always helped when she confided in him. He always knew the right thing to say, and the right time to say it. He and her grandmother had that in common. Chrissie inhaled deeply, then confessed. "I met a guy tonight."

Appearing stunned, William closed his eyes. "We've talked about this, Peanut. You know how dangerous it is for us to get too attached to a mortal."

Though Chrissie knew he was right, she couldn't help striking out at him. "That's why I never tell you anything. You find fault with everything I do!" That wasn't true. She told her dad almost everything. He was the most understanding father any girl could ask for. Still, she couldn't stop herself from lashing out.

The pain in his eyes was unmistakable, and she wanted to apologize to him. However, her remorse ended when William made the mistake of saying, "Sweetheart, it isn't right for you to get involved with a human."

"Humph, wasn't it your idea for me to enroll in college and behave like any other female. Wasn't it you who said let's not hide anymore. Let's get back out in the world?" Chrissie wielded his words like a sword against him. Twisting her verbal knife, she pierced her father's very soul. "I never understood why I had to be separated from the world for seven years anyway."

He closed his eyes against her. "You're right, and I do want you to experience those things," his voice broke, "but I don't want you to do it at the expense of a life."

Losing her resolve, Chrissie lowered her head. "It doesn't matter anyway. I said I met a guy. That doesn't mean he's interested in me."

"Sweetheart," William stroked her hand, "he would be a fool not to be interested in you. You're a beautiful young woman, and I know how isolated you have been, since..." He hesitated before he went on. "I know you think I'm too hard on you, but I know the temptations out there. We're living in a world where we don't belong. One slip could be fatal for an innocent person. You wouldn't want that, would you?"

"I know that you worry about me, but you don't have to. I know the consequences of my actions, and I'm not going to do anything that would jeopardize you, or me." The words sounded hollow even as she spoke them.

"I'm not worried about me." William pressed his lips together. "I'm worried about you, about how you would feel if you fell in love with a human, then ended up destroying him." Each of his words beseeched her to understand.

Guilt-ridden because of her behavior, Chrissie acquiesced. "I've got it, Dad. I'll be good. I promise I won't see him again." She shrugged. "He's just a guy, no biggie."

This was a promise she had already broken in her heart. She couldn't stay away from Dylan. She'd never felt that way before. At the risk of hurting her dad, she committed to be true to herself. Chrissie stood and looked up the stairs. Peering over her shoulder, she added. "By the way, I hung out at the Shack all evening. I think it would be a great investment."

"Thanks, baby." William's expression softened.

Thoughts of Dylan were already overwhelming her. She sprinted up the stairs for the privacy of her bedroom.

CHAPTER THREE

First Date

Careful not to damage her car by hitting speed bumps, Chrissie took her time creeping over the campus parking lot. There were no unoccupied spaces near Jefferson Hall, so she circled the lot several times before she spotted a blue truck pulling out of a space. As she waited for the vehicle to exit, Chrissie felt anxious about her first night of class. Not that she feared failing a class; that was the least of her worries. Because she didn't make friends easily, she felt uncomfortable in unfamiliar surroundings.

A trooper from birth, she never let her inherent shyness stop her from doing anything she wanted to do. Like an actor taking the stage for the first time, Chrissie had learned her lines and prepared herself to take center stage. Unfortunately, she remained a bit fretful about facing this new juncture. Only one positive aspect soothed her misgivings—Dylan. Even if she didn't have an opportunity to see him, the knowledge of his close proximity comforted her. Suddenly, someone shouted, "Hey. I didn't expect to see you here tonight. I was going to call you when I got home."

Chrissie tilted her head forward as she recognized the deep resounding voice. The truck vacated the parking spot, and she pulled in. Starry-eyed, she watched as Dylan strolled in her direction. Pushing the switch to lower the window, she asked, "Hi. I didn't expect to see you either. What are you doing here?"

Dylan leaned down and peered into her window. "I have a class from four until five-thirty on Tuesdays and Thursdays. Professor Sterling let us out a little late today. What about you?"

With a little too much enthusiasm, she responded, "My science class is on Tuesdays from six until nine." She reached for the handle to open the door, but Dylan was already opening it for her. She grabbed her books and got out of the car. Dylan took the books from her hands. "Are you going straight home after class?"

Remembering what she had promised her father, Chrissie stared at the ground. "I had planned to. Why?" She elevated her eyes until they met his gaze. "What did you have in mind?"

Dylan shrugged. "I thought we could go to the Shack and grab a couple of burgers."

"Humph, burgers, I'm not a big burger fan. What else do they serve?"

He seemed amused and chuckled. "You know, just the regular stuff."

"Maybe I'll just have a cup of herbal tea," she replied quietly.

With narrowed eyes, Dylan seemed somewhat puzzled. "How old did you say you were?"

"I'm twenty-five. Is that a problem?"

"Nah. Herbal tea is the kind of thing my mom would order."

Anger surged inside her—well, more embarrassment than anger. "I see. Well, if you think I'll embarrass you in front of your friends, we don't have to go." She yanked her books from his hands and turned. "I've got to go. I'll be late for class." Her temper was quicker now than it used to be before her transformation. She had always been feisty, but now, she erupted at the slightest provocation. Her dad said that would change with time. The stress of interacting with humans without attacking them, coupled with adjusting to a new environment, made her jumpy.

"Chillax." Dylan grinned at her. "Don't get all salty on me. I wasn't trying to be rude. It has nothing to do with my being embarrassed. I'm sorry if I offended you. I just don't know of another person *our* age, who drinks herb tea." He flashed a smile, then put his hand on her cheek. For the first time, he was serious. "I want to spend some time with you."

Dylan's very presence overwhelmed her. She had only experienced this emotion once before. "N, no," she stammered. "I'm the one who should be sorry. When you get to know me better, you'll learn that I tend to be a little sensitive."

He rubbed his arm through his shirtsleeve. "Let's start over. Would you like to go to the Shack with me after your class?"

Thinking of herself and forgetting her promise, she smiled. "I would love to go to the Shack with you. I can meet you there after class. Say, around nine-thirty."

"Awesome, I'll see you there. By the way, if you get out early, text me. I don't want you sitting around waiting for me."

"Okay." *How thoughtful.*

He reached for her books once again. "May I?" Chrissie released the books into his care. "Let's walk while we talk. I don't want you to be late for class on your first night."

"I agree." Everything seemed perfect. With Dylan by her side, even facing the unknown would be a pleasure.

However, the euphoria of that moment didn't last. Chrissie cringed when he asked, "When are your other classes? I looked for you all day, but I didn't see you at all."

Not wanting to reveal too much, she stalled before she answered. "All my classes are late in the day. Why were you looking for me?"

"Well. I had such a good time last night that I wanted to see you again. What time's your first class tomorrow?"

"I have English from four-thirty till six."

Jefferson Hall was a few yards from her car, so it didn't take very long to reach the building. Dylan opened the front door for her and held it while she entered. "What room is your class in?"

She fumbled around in her purse and pulled out her class schedule. Not that she needed it; she remembered the entire schedule verbatim. Her dad had said humans don't remember small details like that, so she continued the charade. "Let's see." She bit her lip as she traced the print to the room's number. "I'm in B7."

"Sweet." He enunciated the 't' with extra emphasis. "That's the room right across from my last class. We'll see each other all the time."

They strolled to the door. Dylan accompanied Chrissie into the room, then he took a seat next to her. As Chrissie perused her surrounding, she noticed a multi-colored poster with the phrase ¡Feliz Año Nuevo! on the wall. Next to it, hung a huge black sombrero trimmed in white. Atop the instructor's desk, stood a small cactus plant. "I wonder why there's so much Hispanic paraphernalia in this room."

"Professor Marshall is from Juarez, and proud of it."

She nodded. "Oh." They continued to talk until the professor entered the room.

Once Professor Marshall stood behind the podium, he cleared his throat and scrutinized the room. His thick horned rimmed glasses made him look as blind as a bat. With his hair pulled back into a ponytail, the deep waves in his dark brown hair were clearly visible. However, when he spotted Dylan, his forehead creased into a deep frown. His countenance took on the appearance of utter disgust. Turning up his nose, he asked, "Mr. Duncan, are you planning to take my class again this semester? I realize my course presented a challenge to you, but you *did* pass. So, why are you here?"

Dylan beamed and sprang from his chair. "Just leaving, Professor Marshall. Far be it from me to interrupt your students' education. I realize how much they're looking forward to your *interesting* lectures, sir. I could hardly contain my enthusiasm when I was in your class." The entire room broke into a roar of laughter, and Chrissie snickered as well. At that, Dylan sauntered toward the door. Standing in the hallway, he gazed at her and nodded.

It was an understatement that Dylan's presence perturbed Professor Marshall. He glared daggers at Chrissie, flipped open his computer and called the roll. When he came to her name, he glanced up. His expression made her rather uncomfortable. "Are you Professor Garrett's daughter?"

"Y, yes, sir," she stammered, feeling a bit self-conscious.

Professor Marshall rolled his eyes at her and grumbled, "Interesting."

As expected, Marshall's lecture was as dry as a dust storm in the middle of the Sahara. The class dragged by. Now, she understood Dylan's ridicule. Pretending to take notes, she flipped open her spiral. Her hand had a life of its own. Pictures of cartoon characters she loved in her youth chased each other across the page. Bored with her artistic endeavor, she closed her notebook. When she thought she could take the endless drone no longer, she heard Kaylee's voice mentioning her name from behind her. Dylan's presence had captivated her attention so much; she hadn't noticed the other young women in the back of the classroom. Unable to resist, she focused her attention on the conversation.

Kaylee mumbled under her breath to the person sitting next to her. "I saw them in the Shack last night. I don't know what he sees in her." Acid dripped from every syllable.

The woman beside her replied, "Don't worry about it, Kaylee. You know how guys are. Anyway, you're not seeing Dylan anymore, are you? I thought the two of you broke up six months ago."

With great pride, Kaylee proclaimed, "We still see each other from time to time."

As she rubbed the back of her neck, Chrissie pondered. *"I wonder if she intended for me to overhear that."*

Barely audible, Kaylee's friend added, "I don't know why you continue to see him. He tells everyone you're a pest. Why do you continue to put yourself through that?"

"You've never been in love, Amanda, so you wouldn't understand. When's the last time you had a date anyway?"

"I may not be dating right now, but I do have some pride. I wouldn't stoop to throwing myself at someone who has made it clear he doesn't want me anymore." Chrissie could hear the hurt in Amanda's voice. She wanted to walk to the back of the room and rip both of Kaylee's arms from their sockets. "Besides," Amanda continued, "you have to admit, she is rather pretty."

Chrissie didn't know whether she said it because she felt that way, or if she used the information to annoy Kaylee. Whatever the reason, her words struck their target.

"So. You really think she's pretty, huh?" Kaylee fumed loud enough for the entire class to hear.

Amanda sneered and twisted the knife. "Well, Kaylee, you have to admit she's no dog." The corners of Chrissie's lips inched upwards, and she glowed.

"I think you need to get your eyes checked. She looks like she hasn't seen the sun in years." Kaylee seethed with jealousy, and Chrissie understood why Dylan had broken up with her.

Although Chrissie realized it was petty of her, she felt resentment rising inside of her. Like any other human female, she wanted to scratch Kaylee's eyes out. The problem, however, was that she wasn't human, and if provoked, her attack could be lethal.

Growing up, Chrissie had a problem with self-esteem. Her mother died when she was ten, and she never knew her father. Chrissie always thought her dad was ashamed of her, and that's why he left them. As a result, when anyone had issues with her, she reverted into that lost little girl.

"Miss Kaylee Ford," Marshall boomed, disrupting their conversation. "Would you like to answer the question I posed to the class?" Chrissie wasn't the only one listening to their little tête-à-tête. "If I am not mistaken, you enrolled in this class to listen to my lecture, not to visit with Miss Caldwell." The cynicism rolled off his tongue, and his scathing remarks pleased Chrissie.

"I'm sorry, sir. I'm afraid I wasn't paying attention," Kaylee admitted.

"Yes, Miss Ford, you are sorry." He stepped from behind his podium. "The next time you want to have a discussion with Miss Caldwell, take it outside."

Kaylee sprang from her seat. "Who do you think you're talking to?" She retorted aloud. Her nose wriggled as though she smell a foul stench. Under her breath, she mumbled, "You probably still have your leaf blower in your trunk." Students in close proximity snickered.

Professor Marshall turned his lip upward into a snarl. "Sit down, Miss Ford."

With her hands on her hips, Kaylee advanced in his direction. "How dare you tell me what to do. I'm not an urchin who sells tamales on the sidewalk to make a living."

"Get out." He narrowed his eyes. "And I mean, stay out. Don't come back into my classroom. Ever." Professor Marshall tapped his foot as he watched Kaylee gather her belongings. When she stormed past, he slammed his book shut. Obviously annoyed by the caustic confrontation, Marshall glanced at his watch, scanned the room, and then said, "Class is dismissed."

Professor Marshall had dismissed class twenty minutes early. Still angered by Kaylee's exhibition, Chrissie pretended to collect her things. Once everyone had filed by, she stood to leave. Frowning, she cut her eyes toward the front desk. She could feel Professor Marshall's eyes ogling her. No teacher had ever looked at her like that before, and she dreaded passing him. "Miss Garrett," he called as she attempted to exit the room. "May I have a word with you?"

Chrissie didn't know what he wanted, but being alone with him made her uneasy. "Yes, sir."

"It may be none of my business, but I was wondering..." He paused for a second before he asked, "Does your father know you're seeing, Mr. Duncan?"

"Excuse me?" Fury erupted inside her. She felt as though steam was escaping her ears. It always infuriated her when she felt someone was being slandered, especially someone for whom she had feelings. Trying to contain her rage, she gritted her teeth before she answered, "I don't see how that's any of your business, sir. I'm your student, but that doesn't give you the right to interfere in my personal life."

"I understand that, Miss Garrett, but your father is my co-worker, and I would hate to see his daughter involved with someone like that."

Chrissie's fury intensifying, she retorted, "And just what do you mean by, *someone like that*?"

Marshall sighed. "Mr. Duncan is renowned for his rather unorthodox sense of humor, as well as his insincerity." He marched around his desk. "And to be quite frank, Miss Garrett, he also has a reputation as the campus Casanova. He's the kind who calls attention to himself, and by association, he can call unwanted attention to you."

In order to restrain her temper, Chrissie had to bite the inside of her cheek, causing herself intense pain. "Professor Marshall, I appreciate your concern, but I'm a big girl, and I can take care of myself. I believe it's my business if I want to call attention to myself."

Marshall stepped backwards, but studied Chrissie's eyes. "You are a young woman, and as such, you have much to lose by becoming involved with Duncan. He's not right for you. If Miss Ford wants to lower herself by being involved with someone like him, that's one thing, but I will not stand idly by while he takes advantage of you."

She could no longer contain the wrath. "Wait. One. Minute. I don't know who you think you are, but you have no right to tell me how to live my life. I don't even know you." When Chrissie realized she had wagged her finger in Professor Marshall's face, shock filled her soul. "You had better stay out of my business, or I swear you will regret it."

A faint growl emanated from deep inside Professor Marshall's chest. At that instant, she peered into his eyes. Much to her dismay, she noticed almost imperceptible red rings surrounding his irises, spheres that would have gone undetected by a human. Then, she realized he had more than a passing interest in what she did, or said. But, that didn't explain why he seemed vested in whom she dated. Chrissie whirled around, then sprinted from the room.

As she bolted down the corridor, Chrissie wondered, *"What just happened, here? How could I have missed the red rings in his eyes?"* She wasn't that careless, or at least she didn't think she was. *"How could I not recognize another vampire in my presence?"*

Vampires have a very distinctive odor, different from humans, but Professor Marshall smelled human. *"Dad told me I needed to hone my skills, but this is ridiculous."*

Her confidence shaken and upset by their confrontation, Chrissie considered waiting for Marshall in the parking lot, attacking him from behind, and ripping him into shreds. Most of the crowd would be gone by then, and those who remained would be hurrying to get home. No one would even miss him. After all, as boring as his class was, she was sure the student body would cheer when he disappeared.

Of course, Chrissie knew she couldn't do that. Not only would he be a formidable opponent, a fact she now realized, but also someone would miss him. More to the point, she would know what she'd done. With stunned emotions, she pushed that idea out of her mind; she had a date to keep. Wow, she had a date to keep. She couldn't wait to see Dylan again, and here she was about to meet him for — for what? What was she meeting him for? What kind of relationship could she ever hope to have with him? At that point, she didn't know or care. Hurriedly, she took her cell from her purse and texted the words, *Oe, otw.* She smiled to herself. *"Out early. On the way."*

When Chrissie exited the building, she was lost in the gruesome carnage of her imagination. Seeing Dylan outside, shocked, and pleased her. Propped against her car, he wore knee length khaki shorts and a black hoodie. His matching Harley cap was turned backwards. In his adorable eyes, Chrissie could see the reflection of the full moon. Wanting to bridge the gap between them, she had to restrain herself from breaking into a sprint. "Hi, I thought we were meeting at the Shack." Was she sounding too eager? What was happening to her? Self-control had been her greatest asset. Nonetheless, where Dylan was involved, she had difficulty governing herself.

"I figured, if old man Marshall reacted to me the way he used to, he would be too annoyed to hold class for the entire time. I decided to wait." He glanced at his watch. "He made it longer than I thought he would." Enjoying his mischief, he chuckled.

"I just texted you to let you know I was on the way, but I'm glad you decided to wait." It occurred to her that most people didn't wear shorts in the winter. "Aren't you cold?"

Dylan raised his brows. "Cold?"

"As in wearing shorts in this weather?"

"Oh. Cold." He shook his head. "Nope." His eyes shifted from left to right. "Uh. I spilled a drink on my jeans. These shorts were in my truck, so I just threw them on instead of going back to my apartment to change." He glanced down. "Besides, no matter how cold it is outside, my legs never get cold."

"That's odd," she mused.

He grinned, and then joked, "East Texas is so hot during the summer, that it takes until January before you cool off."

Dylan's humor was rich. She smiled anxious to start their date. "Are you ready to go? Do you want me to follow you there?"

With a pensive expression, Dylan revealed his plan. "I wondered if you'd like to ride with me. I'll bring you back to pick up your car later." His words thrust her mind back in time. Her grandmother told her never to get into cars with men she didn't know. Chrissie's reluctance disappeared. Somehow, Dylan seemed safe.

Just then, Professor Marshall opened the door to Jefferson Hall. Nervous he would overhear their conversation, Chrissie stalled before answering Dylan. Odds were, he had already heard every word they'd said.

"Well, what do you say?" Dylan pressed. Professor Marshall strolled by. Disapproval was evident in his eyes.

Uneasy about Marshall's stares, she stuttered, "S, sure, I think that's a good idea. After all, why take two cars?"

Dylan motioned toward his truck. "Shall we?"

Now, Chrissie understood why Dylan attracted such attention from the women on campus. His raw magnetism was undeniable. Never before had anyone treated her with such chivalry. Opening doors, and carrying books for ladies, went out with the feminist movement. Such a gallant companion proved to be a refreshing change of pace.

CHAPTER FOUR

Test

It appeared they'd arrived at the Shack during the busiest part of the evening. The place was packed. When they entered, several people yelled, "What's up, Dill?"

As Dylan escorted Chrissie to the booth near the rear, he nodded and waved. "Is this booth okay?"

"This is fine." The establishment didn't stand on protocol, and they could seat themselves.

Dylan helped Chrissie remove her tan buckskin jacket. He laid it over the back of the seat. Then, he took off his jacket and tossed it in the seat beside him. When he sat down, he stretched and placed his arms behind his head.

Chrissie peered at his right arm, and then his left. She rubbed the tip of her nose. "Didn't that dog bite you last night?"

Dylan lowered his arms. He flexed his finger before he gripped his right wrist with his left hand. "It was just a scratch." He rotated his wrist. "You can't even see it anymore."

"Um. I could have sworn..." She scratched her head. *"I know that dog bit him. Yet, there's not a mark on his arm. Humph."*

The waitress bounced over to their booth. "What'll it be tonight, Dylan?"

Dylan didn't bother to look at the menu board. "I'm going to have a steak with all the trimmings. Make it blood rare." He glanced at Chrissie. "What will you have?"

"I'm not hungry, but I am a little chilly. I'll have some herbal tea." She knew full well her choices were limited to three things: water, herb tea and soda. However, she didn't like the way soda felt when it hit her stomach.

"Are you sure that's all you want?" Dylan leaned toward her. "I'm buying."

"I'm sure." She glanced at Jena sheepishly. "I'm not a very big eater." Chrissie was self-conscious about her eating habits, or the lack thereof. A lie would suffice.

"Well," he kidded, "if you plan to hang around me, we'll have to see what we can do about that." He elevated his eyes toward their waitress, Jena. "Jena, did I hear something about this place being sold?"

Chrissie cringed. Her dad had signed the papers that morning. Since she felt out of step with everyone else at school, she chose not to tell anyone she owned the establishment, not even Dylan.

"Yeah, that's what Ernie says. He says Mr. Fletcher already has a buyer."

Dylan frowned. "Do you know who bought it?"

Jena shook her head. "No. But some contractors are supposed to come out and look at the place in a couple of days."

"I hope they don't make too many changes." Dylan scoffed. "I like the place the way it is."

"Me too." As she flitted away, Jena peered over her shoulder. "I'll be back with you order in a couple of minutes."

Dylan spread his arms across the back of his seat. His long limbs covered its expanse.

Unable to think of an original icebreaker, Chrissie utilized the classic conversation opener. "So. What's your major?"

"Isn't that line a bit passé? If you want to start a conversation, try something more original." Her expression must have given away her hurt. "We can talk about anything," he added. "You don't need to make small talk." He reached across the table and stroked her hand.

Struggling to regain her composure, Chrissie focused on the patterns in the wooden tabletop. The touch of his hand thrilled her more than any other she had ever known. "Dylan. It takes time for me to feel at ease with most people."

This time Dylan appeared wounded. "You didn't have any trouble last night. We talked like we'd known each other for years. So, what happened?"

"Last night wasn't planned. It just happened. Neither of us had any expectations, but tonight is more like a date." The memory of Professor Marshall's words burned fresh in her mind, and how could she forget Kaylee's little performance?

"I don't know. You act as if something is bothering you. Is it something you can't share?" For someone who hadn't known her very long, Dylan seemed to understand her quite well.

She contemplated that thought for a moment and then decided to discuss her concerns with him. "To tell you the truth, Dylan, Professor Marshall stopped me after class and warned me that you're something of a Casanova."

Dylan's nostrils flared, and he clenched his fist. Chrissie detected an increase in his heart rate. "What business is it of his? Who does he think he is?"

Watching Dylan's wild behavior, Chrissie smirked. *"Nice to know he also has something of a temper."* Everyone in the room gawked at them. Dylan reacted with such intensity that she wondered whether she should have told him about Marshall's odd opinion. In an attempt to defuse the situation, she spoke as soothing as possible, "I'm sorry I brought it up. Let's talk about something else."

The muscles in his jaw flexed. "What else did he tell you?" he demanded.

"Nothing important, he just said you're different, but you already told me that." She chuckled as she twisted one of her ringlets. "I rather enjoy your unusual way of looking at the world."

The results worked better than she'd anticipated. Dylan's muscles relaxed and his respiration returned to normal. "Look, Chrissie. I'm not pretending to be a saint. There have been other women in my life. I won't lie to you about that, but I like you. We hit it off so well last night. You're the first person I've been open with since my dad passed away." His voice escalated, building with intensity. "Marshall tried to poison your mind against me. That's inexcusable. He had no right to say anything to you."

Astonished by the force of his words, Chrissie stumbled, "I, I'm sorry I shouldn't have mentioned it to you. I don't know why I did."

"I'm glad you did. I needed to know." Peering into her eyes, he took her breath away. "I don't know what's going to happen with us, but I want to explore the possibilities. You're most interesting. The others are just worthless drones."

Hearing Dylan's confession, Chrissie exploded with joy. The idea that he cared overwhelmed her.

For a moment, she was speechless. When she regained her poise, she gushed. "I feel the same way."

He slid his hand across the table and placed it atop hers. No longer did anger burn in his eyes. On the contrary, it was replaced by tenderness. Chrissie had to contain herself when he murmured, "Your hair is gorgeous. I love the way it falls into ringlets around your face." He leaned in close to her. "What color are your eyes? Your pupils are light brown, but your irises explode into green starbursts. I've never seen eyes that color before."

As if sent to break the spell, a group of students marched over to their table and began chatting. Dylan made the introductions, pointing to each person. "Christina, this is Matt Jenkins, Estefina Garcia, Jeffery Weldon and Amanda Caldwell. Guys, this is Christina Garrett."

Chrissie recognized Amanda from class. She felt grateful that Amanda had defended her against Kaylee. Amanda was tall and slender. She had blonde hair and blue eyes. Though she wasn't a beauty, she was passable. Still upset by what transpired in class, Chrissie glanced up shyly and greeted them. "Hello."

Amanda must have felt a little uncomfortable as well. She feigned a smile. "Hi," she mumbled. Chrissie noticed she was careful not to meet her eyes.

Estefina broke the ice. "I heard you're a freshman. Are you enjoying college life so far?" Estefina scooted into the booth next to Dylan and motioned for Amanda to take the seat next to Chrissie.

Chrissie didn't like the idea of Amanda sitting close to her, but she retained her composure and focused on Estefina's question. "It has been rather interesting so far. I attended my first class today. Professor Marshall is somewhat eccentric to say the least." She laughed.

Estefina folded her arms. "Yeah, I have heard he's a little weird." Her jet-black hair flowed loosely about her flawless brown skin. "I haven't had him yet. I'm a freshman myself. I'll take science next semester. What other classes do you have?"

"I'm taking the basics. You know, English, math, economics, science."

Matt, had been scrutinizing Chrissie's face since he walked up. "Are you related to Professor Garrett?"

Chrissie nodded.

Dylan glanced at him and answered, "Yeah, he's her dad."

"Professor Garrett is your dad?" Jeffery grumbled. "I failed economics last semester, and I've got to take it again next semester."

"You should have gone to class once in a while," Dylan teased. "Those late nights you spent partying didn't help your grades."

"When do you have English?" Estefina interrupted.

Chrissie tapped her foot against the leg of the booth. "…on Mondays and Wednesdays, from four-thirty till six."

"Awesome! So do I. Why don't you sit by me in class? We can be study partners. I'm told that Mrs. Phillips is a real task master."

Chrissie had just met Estefina, and already she liked her. The idea of having a study partner was delightful. Although she didn't need a study buddy, she really could use a friend. "That would be great."

Estefina turned to Amanda." Have you had Professor Marshall yet?"

Amanda focused on the floor. She tried to hide her discomfort, but it was obvious. "I'm taking science this semester."

Chrissie couldn't resist testing the waters. "I saw you in class tonight. Professor Marshall called on the girl you were sitting with."

She nodded without saying a word.

"What's her name?" Chrissie pressed. She needed to determine Amanda's reaction to what happened in class.

"Her name's Kaylee Ford. Why don't you ask Dylan about her? He knows her very well."

Dylan rested his head on the back of the seat. "Yeah, I saw the two of you in the room when I walked Chrissie to class."

"I heard she got kicked out of class today." Estefina's bubbly personality shined through even when she spoke of negative matters.

Amanda ogled Chrissie viciously. "She did."

Jeffery, who had evidently grown bored with the conversation, patted Amanda on the shoulder. "Let's go hang out in the game room."

"Good idea," Matt agreed.

Gazing into Chrissie's eyes, Dylan declared, "Not me, I'm going to eat and call it an early night."

The waitress arrived with Dylan's food just as Jeffery elbowed Matt in the ribs. When he had his attention, Jeffery raised his brows. "Right. Well, we'll see you tomorrow," Jeffery declared. The innuendos streamed from each syllable. "Let's go girls." He grinned.

Apparently, thankful for the opportunity to escape, Amanda bounced up, but Estefina lingered momentarily. "I'll see you in class tomorrow." She stood up.

Once the couple was alone, they sat in silence. Dylan dined on blood rare steak and a baked potato. This time, he chewed his food without haste, unlike the burger he devoured the night before. Chrissie wrapped her hand around her cup of tea and allowed the steam to rise into her face. The aroma tickled her senses.

When Dylan had finished his meal, he leaned in close to her. "Are you ready to go?"

Disappointed, Chrissie sighed. She didn't want the night to end. "Sure, if you are."

"I thought we could take a drive. I want to show you the town. It's quite beautiful at night."

Again her grandmother's voice echoed in Chrissie's ear, but she ignored the sage advice. "That would be nice." A part of her wondered exactly what he had in mind. Taken by his charisma, she couldn't resist spending more time with him.

CHAPTER FIVE

Doubts

Dylan pointed out all the local landmarks as they drove through the city. He was right. The city was breathtaking at night. Every street was adorned with left over holiday decorations. Each building was draped in a different color: red, green, blue, and purple. The county courthouse sparkled with twinkling white lights. A gingerbread house with candy canes and lollipops decorated the front of a local business.

When they reached the town square, Dylan pulled into a spot and parked. He angled his body to face Chrissie, then placed his arm on the steering wheel. "How do you like the sights?"

Chrissie scanned the surrounding area and marveled. "It's breathtaking."

Without warning, his face turned serious. "What happened in class tonight?"

Taking in his grave demeanor, she gasped. "Nothing important."

"Then why did you make a point of mentioning it to Amanda?"

"Well, she and Kaylee were talking during Professor Marshall's lecture. He called them on it." She rubbed her arm. "He was pretty hard on Kaylee." Chrissie scanned the roof of the car. "*At least I won't have to deal with her every other day.*" Turning her head to the left, she refocused on Dylan. "I was just curious..."

"Curious about what?" he pressed.

"I don't know." She shrugged. "I guess I wanted to see your reaction when I mentioned her name."

"Are you in the habit of playing games with people?" His voice hardened as he spoke.

It never occurred to her that he'd think she was playing games. "What are you talking about?"

"I told you I broke up with Kaylee six months ago. Why did you feel the need to put Amanda on the spot like that?"

"If you must know, she and Kaylee were talking about me." She stared out the windshield. "I overheard the conversation." Turning back to him, she added curtly, "Professor Marshall must have heard it too; he intervened."

"Is that why he told you those things about me?" Anger burned in his words.

"I don't know. I don't know him that well."

"Is he a friend of your father's?"

"They work together, so I'm sure they're cordial to each other. Why?"

"Because. I'm trying to figure out why he's so interested in you."

"Maybe it has nothing to do with me." Chrissie softened her voice. "Maybe it's because he doesn't like anyone talking in his class while he's trying to lecture."

"Or maybe, he has something lovely in his eye."

Chrissie waved her hand. "Don't be ridiculous. I just met the man tonight."

"You met me yesterday, but here you sit." Sarcasm dripped from his tone. He clenched his sparkling white teeth. Chrissie could see their sharp points.

Ignoring her find, she glared at him and grimaced. "What are you trying to say, Dylan?"

"I'm saying—" He used his fingers to make quotation marks on the air. "He seems too concerned about someone who's '*just*' a student."

Too angry to discuss it further, Chrissie folded her arms and glared out the side window. "I don't want to talk about this anymore."

Dylan stared at her. When he spoke again, his voice was almost melodic. "You're right. We should find something else to talk about." Chrissie said nothing. Anger fueled her silence. "By the way, where are you from? You don't sound like a typical Texan."

Although perturbed, she answered him courteously. "I'm from Pinole, California."

"How long did you live there?"

"All my life."

With a soft, even inflection, Dylan asked, "You told me you and your dad traveled a lot. Did you have to move around because of his job? I know professors don't tend to stay in the same place for too many years."

"No, I was raised by my maternal grandmother." Though Chrissie endeavored to resist his allure, she thawed. "I didn't meet my father until I was sixteen." She lied, but she couldn't tell him the truth.

He widened his eyes. "Really?"

"Yes, my father and mother weren't married. After my mother died, my nana took the responsibility of bringing me up." She didn't know why, but more information than she'd planned to reveal came pouring out of her mouth.

"Does your grandmother still live in Pinole?"

"Yeah." Thinking about her grandmother was always bittersweet. She loved the memories of growing up in her house. The realization that she'd never feel her nana's hand as they talked at the kitchen table saddened her.

As though he could read her mind, Dylan rubbed her shoulder. "Do you miss her?"

She smiled. "Very much, I went to live with her and my grandfather when I was ten years old. Grandpa died a year later." Without blinking, she stared into empty space. "So Nana and I are very close."

He bent in her direction. "If you don't mind my asking, how did you come to live with your dad?"

Chrissie drew in a breath. "A couple of years ago, I was diagnosed with cancer. I almost died. During that time, my dad came to see me. We've been together ever since."

"Wow." Dylan scanned her from head to foot. "You don't look like you've ever been sick a day in your life."

"I'm not anymore." She turned to face him. "The cancer is gone."

"Do you ever worry about it coming back?"

"Never. There's no chance of that. The doctors say I'm one hundred percent cured."

"There's always a chance it could come back." Dylan's gentle words reflected his deep concern for her well being. He paused and then changed the subject. "Can I ask you something?"

"Yes," she replied remotely. She had shared her most painful memories with him. There was no reason to hold back now.

"Why did your grandmother let you go?"

Chrissie shrugged. "I guess Nana realized I needed to know my father." That was also a lie. Her grandmother didn't know what happened to her body. All Nana knew was that Chrissie's died and her body disappeared. "She's very generous like that." That part was true. Her grandmother would sacrifice her happiness for Chrissie's without a thought.

Dylan draped his arm over the steering wheel and gazed at her. "She must be an incredible woman."

"She is, but let's talks about you now. Where are you from?"

"You wouldn't recognize the name if I told you. It's a very small village."

"Try me."

Dylan made no comment for a long moment. He seemed lost in thought. When he did speak, he changed the subject once again. "I love coming down here and looking at the lights."

Careening her neck, Chrissie peered through the windshield. "I'm glad we came. Everything is so pretty."

"I told you the city was gorgeous at night. Speaking of gorgeous, your eyes are beautiful." Chrissie heard his heartbeat quicken. As he continued to scrutinize her eyes, his mouth dropped open, and he pointed toward her face. "You have the slightest red rings around your irises."

No other human had ever noticed the red in her eyes before, and she sat in awe of the irony. Here she was, a creature known for mental and physical acuity. Yet, Dylan had noticed quite a few things about her. Was she missing something about him?

Chrissie scratched her head. *Humph, I must be slipping.* Wanting to offer some reasonable rationalization, she explained, "My mother had deep brown eyes, and my father has green eyes, so the combination of the two gives you hazel." What explanation could she give about the red? She processed the information and lied, "I have bad allergies. I'm allergic to almost every kind of tree in East Texas. I guess that's why my eyes have a reddish cast."

He nodded and raised a brow. "Humph, I suppose." Looking somewhat apprehensive, he put his index finger on his lips, and then inspected her face. After a moment of what seemed like profound contemplation he spoke abruptly. "Let's get you back to your car."

The silence in the car was deafening. She wondered what he'd seen that caused his reaction. But, she dared not ask for fear of what she might learn. Chrissie broke the silence. "Will I see you tomorrow?"

As Dylan glanced at her, he grunted, "Sure. I'll see you tomorrow evening.

CHAPTER SIX

Confrontation

On the drive home, Chrissie considered all that transpired during the course of the evening. It must have been her imagination. Dylan couldn't suspect anything. She'd been so careful.

Once she pulled into the driveway and parked, she caught her breath. Before she opened the car door, she heard a conversation inside the house that she'd rather avoid. Professor Marshall was discussing what happened in class with her dad.

Chrissie unlocked the door as quietly as possible. Could she manage to get up the stairs without attracting their attention? Aware it was a wasted endeavor, she eased the door up on its hinges to prevent it from making contact with the floor. Her father's ears were sharper than most, not even a vampire could escape their acuity.

"Christina," he yelled from his den. "Come into the study please. We need to talk to you." Why did she bother to attempt the subterfuge? They'd both heard her engine anyway.

"Man," she mumbled. Chrissie knew what it meant when her father used her full name. She inhaled to steel herself against the quarrel she knew would ensue, and then strolled into the room. "Yes, Father?"

"Christina, Walter tells me you're seeing Dylan Duncan. Is there any truth to this?" His face was a mass of concern and disappointment.

Avoiding her father's gaze, she turned to Professor Marshall. Chrissie greeted him with unexpected civility, though she desired nothing more than to slash open his face. "Hello Professor Marshall. I didn't expect to see you here tonight."

"Christina," her father repeated with more force. "I asked you a question. I expect you to answer me at once. "William seldom raised his voice. What had Marshall told him?

The notion of Marshall interfering in her life infuriated her. Anger surged through every fiber of her being. "Father. When your guest leaves, I will talk to you. I have no intention of discussing my personal life in front of a stranger."

Professor Marshall interjected his views on what he seemed to deem inappropriate behavior. "Miss Garrett, I know it's none of my business, but your actions will not only impact you and your father, it will also affect me. I have no intentions of standing by and allowing a childish crush to ruin all I've built these last five years."

Chrissie narrowed her eyes. "Why are *you* so concerned about me? What I do with my life has nothing to do with you." She found herself taking a defensive stance, ready to attack if the need arose.

"Young lady, we depend upon each other to protect our anonymity. When one of us is exposed, it makes it that much more difficult for the rest of us to maintain our secrecy." Marshall spoke to her as though she were his child.

Sarcasm rolled off her tongue. "Why do you care about secrecy? After all, aren't you a superior creature? Can't you do whatever you want?"

He furrowed his brow. "It isn't a question of what you are capable of doing. It's a question of decorum."

"If you cared about decorum," she growled, "you wouldn't be here now. You don't know me, and you have the unmitigated gall to inject yourself into my affairs."

The word affairs appeared to strike a nerve. Marshall's face hardened. "Even if it wasn't inappropriate for you to be involved with a human, Mr. Duncan would be the worst possible choice."

Chrissie folded her arms. "Your animosity toward Dylan borders on obsession. Why do you dislike him so much?"

William, who she feared was ashamed of her by now, regained his composure and interrupted her. "Christina! I will talk to you later." Her father's displeasure resounded in each syllable.

Chrissie turned to flee the room. More than anything, she wanted out of Marshall's presence. However, she couldn't resist taking one last shot at him. With a smirk, she looked over her shoulder and sneered. "See you tomorrow, Professor."

Obviously mortified, William closed his eyes and growled. "Christina, go now."

Chrissie feared she'd pushed her luck too far, so she fled the room. There would be a heavy toll extracted for her arrogance. Once she entered her bedroom, she sat down behind her desk and listened to the rest of their conversation.

"Walter, I apologize for my daughter's behavior. Christina isn't usually this disrespectful."

As they said goodbye, Marshall offered his unsolicited advice. "You don't need to apologize, William. Nevertheless, you do need to take her in hand. Exert some parental control, if you will. Young women need proper guidance."

"Thank you for your concern, but it would be better if you leave now. Give me an opportunity to speak with her alone." Chrissie could tell by her father's strained statement that he was irritated.

As they made their way to the front door, they continued to discuss her. The creak of the floorboards gave away their position. "The young need a firm hand." Professor Marshall's croaked. His frustration remained evident. "I know she's a young adult. But, perhaps, you should shorten her chain. It's obvious you've given her too many liberties. "

William's voice became more forceful. "Really, Walter, you do presume too much. How I handle Chrissie's behavior is between her and me. She's not a child, for Pete's sake."

"No. She's not a child. And, that's why she's so dangerous to us. If I were you, I'd put a stop to this nonsense before it develops into something more serious." Marshall's tone sounded threatening. Chrissie wondered why he cared so much. While it's true, their actions do affect one another, his reaction to her friendship with Dylan bordered on bizarre.

Chrissie shook with fury, and she thought she'd scream. As if sensing his daughter's stress, William came to her defense. "I will admit that Chrissie's behavior was atrocious, but she was right about one thing. This is a family matter, and we will resolve it as a family."

"I hope you will be able to resolve it." Chrissie heard Marshall say. "There is something odd about that young man—something dangerous. He's not like any other student I've ever had, human or vampire."

"You're beginning to sound like a superstitious mortal." Her father's remarks about humans surprised her. He was usually much more tolerant of differences. "I'll handle the situation from here on out," William insisted. The heavy door groaned as it opened.

"I'm telling you, William, this Duncan bears watching. He's not to be trusted with a beautiful, impressionable young woman like your daughter."

"I'll handle it, Walter."

"Very well, see that you do. Good night."

"Good night." William growled and slammed the door shut. Chrissie heard the wind whirl, as he spun around and called her name, "Christina."

"Dang it." Chrissie hoped he'd wait until later to have this discussion. She grumbled under her breath. "What is it?" She didn't need to raise her voice, he heard every word.

"Get down here." Being twenty-five didn't give her solace, she was in deep trouble. Unfair as it may be, her father still thought of her as an eighteen year old girl.

Not wanting to face her dad, Chrissie meandered slowly as she could manage. When she entered the den, William was facing the window.

"Have a seat," he demanded with his back turned.

She sat on the overstuffed leather recliner at the back of the den. Hopefully, this would end soon. Then, she could return to the sanctuary of her own room. William continued to face the window. Three minutes passed. His silence wounded more than any lecture he could have given her. When he faced her, his harsh tone echoed throughout the room. "You lied to me."

"Dad." Chrissie was filled with regret over her deception. "I didn't really lie. Dylan happened to have a class in Jefferson Hall. When I got to the campus, we ran into each other by chance. We started talking, and he asked me to dinner. I didn't see anything wrong with my decision, so I went."

William glared at her in disbelief. "He invited you to dinner? What, pray tell, did you eat?"

"Ha, Ha." She sneered and rolled her eyes. "I had herbal tea."

"How long do you think you can get away without eating anything? At some point, he's going to wonder why you never eat solid food."

"I hadn't thought that far ahead," she admitted.

"You need to consider all the ramifications of this relationship?"

"I know it was unwise to go out with him, Dad. But, I like him. You don't understand what it's like to be alone all the time." Verbalizing her innermost emotions made Chrissie realize how empty she'd felt the last seven years. In high school, she hadn't been popular. She was a good athlete, but she was also the girl with the glasses and the book beneath her arm—geek all the way. But, she did have several close friends. Since her transformation, it had only been her and her dad. Although she loved him with all her heart, that wasn't enough. Inside, she was an ordinary girl, and needed more.

Her trance was broken when she heard her Dad say, "So, what do you know about him? How old is he?"

A scowl creased Chrissie's brow. "He's a junior, so he's around twenty, but I'm not sure. Why?"

"I think I should know who my daughter is interested in, so when people discuss you with me, I don't sound like a clueless idiot."

"You seem to have made up your mind about him, so why does it matter?" Her anger rose again.

William appeared to sense the change in her mood. She could never fool him; he knew her too well. He responded in a soothing manner. "Chrissie, I know how difficult this existence has been. I would be the last person to begrudge you a little happiness. But Walter seems to think there is something abnormal about this young man."

She had calmed until she heard Professor Marshall's name. "You're not being fair. You haven't even met Dylan yet, and you're already passing judgment. If you ask me, there's something strange about Walter Marshall."

He paused for a moment and looked a little embarrassed. "You are twenty-five years old, and I'm going to talk to you like the woman you are." William swallowed hard and continued, "Have you ever considered what would happen if you tried to be intimate with this young man?"

Too embarrassed to look at his face, Chrissie glared into the fireplace. "I don't want to talk about this with you."

"Maybe not, but you need to know the truth. Passion often turns lethal for those whom we love. How do you think I managed to stay away from your mother for all those years? Do you think it was easy for me? I loved her with all my heart."

Chrissie cast her gaze toward the floor and whispered, "I know, Dad."

He cupped his hands together and placed them under his chin as if he needed to give additional thought to his words before voicing them. "When we feel physical passion, we lose all sense of reason. At that point, our true nature surfaces.

"What are you saying?"

"Sweetheart. If you try to make love to him, you will kill him. Our passions strips away our control — we succumb to our baser instincts."

Feeling she had the upper hand, Chrissie exclaimed, "But, being with Dylan doesn't make me thirsty in the least."

"What?" William wrinkled his forehead and gawked in awe. "Are you telling me that he doesn't make you thirsty, *at all*?"

"Yes, I am."

He drew back and stared pensively at her. After a few moments, he spoke. "You're saying you don't even get a tickle in the back of your throat when you're around him."

"Yes." She was more concerned by his reaction.

With a look of amazement, William rested his index finger on his temple and the others beneath his lower lip.

"What's wrong?" she asked, turning to face him.

At first, he made no comment, but then, he blurted, "I want to meet this boy, tonight."

Chrissie gasped. "What? Why?"

"I'm not going to debate the issue with you. Call him, and get him over here, now."

Astonished by the intensity of his reaction, Chrissie complied without thinking. She whipped her cell out of her pocket and pressed Dylan's number on speed dial. He answered on the first ring.

Trying to determine why her father would insist so adamantly upon seeing him, she blubbered, "Dylan, my dad wants to see you right away. I know it's late, but could you come over tonight?"

"Sure," he replied, as though he had been waiting for the call, "I thought I'd be hearing from him."

His calm demeanor further exasperated her. "What's going on? What is it I don't know?" Chrissie's voice trembled with agitation.

"Don't worry about it, Babe. Be there in a sec."

Her mouth fell open as the phone went dead; apprehension overwhelmed her. True, she had noticed several odd things about Dylan, but she couldn't fathom her father's extreme response. When Chrissie looked up, her father had his back turned.

With cell phone in hand, he talked to Professor Marshall. "It seems your misgivings about this young man were well-founded." Professor Marshall made some comment Chrissie didn't hear, to which her father replied, "Yes, come over right away. He will be here in a moment, and we need a plan."

William placed his phone in his pocket, and faced her with a scowl. "Go to your room, Christina. You can listen from there. I don't want you involved in this."

Fury rose inside her and surged through her very core. "Have you lost your mind? I'm not going anywhere." Chrissie pointed her finger in her father's face and growled. "You need to explain what's going on here." She knew she'd regret her reaction later, but at that point, she didn't care.

"There's no time, Christina. I need to ascertain what we're dealing with myself, before I can explain to you."

"Then I'm not leaving this room. I'll admit there are some odd things about Dylan, but..."

Before she finished her statement, Professor Marshall rang the doorbell. William sprinted to the door and unlocked it with such speed, his movements were almost invisible. He and the Professor marched into the den, discussing strategies as they walked.

Her father outlined his plan. "I'll stand on one side of the room while you stand on the other behind me. Protect my flank. If he tries to attack, we'll be able to control the situation."

Professor Marshall agreed. "Together, we should be able to manage whatever situation arises."

Utterly powerless, Chrissie listened in horror. All the while she wondered what could have caused this quandary. Everyone has quirks in his personality, even her dad.

She waited for Dylan to arrive, every nerve in her body on edge. Once again, William tried to reason with her. "Christina, I'd prefer you to wait upstairs. It will be much safer in your room." Alarm was etched in his face.

Remaining defiant, Chrissie dug in her heels. "Whatever this is about, it concerns me as much, or more, than it does you. I refuse to leave this room until I have answers."

"Christina, you need to let us handle this. Walter is right. This young man presents a danger. I won't have you in the middle of an altercation."

Professor Marshall stood in the corner with a convoluted smirk on his face. His arrogance turned her stomach. Because of him and his poison prognostication, they were at odds.

Her need to defend Dylan spilled out. "Dad, I know Dylan. He presents no danger to me."

"You don't know him. You just met him."

"It may have only been two days, but I feel as though I've known him for years."

"The operative words Christina, are *'feel as though.'*"

"Dad, please," she begged. "When Dylan gets here, let me talk to him. What can he do to hurt me? I'm a vampire, the biggest, baddest creature on the planet."

Professor Marshall growled. "There are other creatures out there who are just as lethal as vampires. I think this Dylan may be among that number."

Chrissie ignored him and continued to reason with her father. "Daddy, think about it. He can't do anything to hurt me — not really."

Just as William was beginning to relent, Chrissie heard Dylan's truck turning onto the driveway. The smooth engine came to a halt and seconds later, he rang the doorbell. She remembered thinking to herself, "*No human moves that fast.*"

This time it was she who sprinted to the door. When Chrissie flung the door open, Dylan was leaning against the door frame.

With no outward signs of trepidation, he asked, "Where are they?"

"*How did he know Professor Marshall would be here?*" Saying nothing, she led the way to the den.

Professor Marshall stood erect in the corner of the room. William was crouched in an offensive stance; his paternal instincts seemed to fuel his irrational behavior.

Dylan swaggered into the den, a bit too arrogant for her comfort. He sat down on the overstuffed leather recliner. "So, what do you *people* want from me?" His emphasis on the word people made Chrissie shudder.

Suspecting he knew the truth, she closed her eyes, bit her lip, and then sighed. "Why did you say *people* like that?"

He tilted his head toward her, never taking his eyes off Professor Marshall, as if he surmised the professor was the greater danger. "No offense, Chrissie. But, this is between them and me. You have nothing to do with it. You should go to your room. After all," he grinned, "it isn't like you can't hear everything we say."

The revelation of his knowledge shocked her, but then anger slapped her again. "Did you and Dad rehearse that line?"

Dylan chuckled. "Did your precious daddy tell you to go to your room, too? How ironic."

William relaxed and, straightened his stance. "Who are you?"

"You know who I am. I'm Dylan — Dylan Caliel Duncan." His smug attitude didn't help the atmosphere in the room. Chrissie had already pushed William to his limit. Marshall didn't need an excuse to strike.

Clearly angered by Dylan's demeanor, Professor Marshall interrupted, "Alright, perhaps a better question would be what are you?"

With a mocking grin, Dylan drawled, "Why, I'm just a college student, trying to get my education."

Marshall bellowed, "You are not *just* a college student. You're something unnatural." He too, crouched in an offensive stance.

No longer teasing, Dylan hissed. "Unnatural? You call me unnatural. That's a bad joke."

"Look," William growled. "I want to know who, and what you are. I don't know what you're up to, but when you brought my daughter into this, you made me a part of your world. Now answer the question. Who and what are you?" William clenched his teeth, exposing razor sharp incisors; his muscles were coiled, and ready to strike. Chrissie had always heard that fathers overreact when it comes to their daughters. Under different circumstances, she would have been pleased.

Dylan's narrowed his eyes. They turned the most terrifying shade of green. In a flash, he sprang from the chair, flipped in midair, and landed atop William's desk, all within a split second. Chrissie gasped as she finally accepted Dylan was something more than human, but what? He wasn't a vampire, and she didn't know of another creature with such speed and agility.

Chrissie's father and the Professor reacted in concert. William whirled and prepared to spring, while the Professor leaped toward Dylan from across the room. Before either could complete their movement, Dylan spiraled through the air and stood behind the Professor. The blazing green of his irises were now encased in glowing red embers.

William turned to face Dylan and advanced. Chrissie was overwhelmed by her father's violent response. She'd never seen him react so fiercely.

Although Chrissie was every bit as angry as everyone else in the room, she couldn't afford to lose her temper in this situation. There was too much at stake, so she gathered her wits, and reasoned. In this confrontation, she would need to be the rational one.

Bolting from where she stood near the door, Chrissie positioned her body between her father and Dylan. In an effort to gain control of the situation she shouted, "Stop! What are you doing? This isn't accomplishing anything." For the moment, all three stood frozen, shocked by her reaction. Seizing advantage of the brief respite, Chrissie took a deep breath and turned to face Dylan. "I realize you don't owe any of us an explanation, but I need to understand. What is this all about?"

Dylan peered at her. "Why don't you ask your father?" His glowing eyes started to cool. "He's the one who summoned me here."

She searched Dylan's face for signs of danger. "I didn't ask my father. I asked you."

He growled. "Apparently, your father and the good Professor perceive me as quite dangerous."

Her face softened. She smiled at him. "Well, with those glowing green eyes, you do look rather lethal. However, I think they're rather attractive." Chrissie flirted in hopes her humor would alleviate the tension.

William contorted his face into a massive frown. "*Christina!*"

Professor Marshall grumbled. "Humph."

Their critical response evidently amused Dylan. He looked at Chrissie and then chuckled. "If I'd known you'd respond like this, I would've gotten angry when we first met."

Ignoring the gawking eyes across the room, Chrissie smirked. "I beg to differ. I've seen specks of green in your eyes already."

Her father gasped at her flippant remark.

Dylan grinned, placed his hands on his lapel and crooned. "For you, I'll explain, but not here, and not now."

Perplexed, but pleased at the thought of being alone with him, Chrissie asked, "When, and where?"

"Go for a ride with me. I'll explain everything."

Before she could respond, Marshall took a step forward. "Oh no, you don't. You're not going anywhere alone with him."

Angry, Chrissie furrowed her brow. She pointed her finger as close to Marshall's face as she could without touching him. "Don't tell me what to do. You don't even know me. What gives you the right to comment one way or the other about anything I do?"

A growl rumbled deep in his chest, but he said nothing.

William scowled and moved toward her. "Well, I do know you, Christina Garrett, and you're not leaving this house with that mutant."

Chrissie had no desire to hurt her father; she had put him through enough. She walked to him and took his hand in hers. "I'll be fine, Daddy. Dylan poses no danger to me."

Professor Marshall interrupted. "With all due respect, Christina." That was the first time Professor Marshall called her by her first name. "You don't know any more about this young man than we do. This could be a trap to get you alone—unprotected." His calm inflection masked the irritation that lurked just beneath the surface.

Dylan placed his hand on her shoulder. "It's your decision, Chrissie."

"I'll go with you," she replied, anxious to get Dylan away from there. Now, she'd find answers to her questions. "Dad," she pleaded, knowing his thoughts. "Please don't follow us."

"Christina." William tightened his fist. "I forbid you to leave this house." The fury in her father's voice stunned her. He had never spoken that harshly before.

Nevertheless, she held her ground. "Dad, I may have stopped aging at eighteen, but I am twenty-five. This is my decision." Chrissie felt awful for speaking to her father in that way, especially in front of Marshall. Dylan reached for her hand, and she marched away.

Hand in hand, they strolled to the door. As they stepped into the night, Chrissie heard Marshall's growl. "You shouldn't have allowed her to leave with him. You don't know what he's capable of doing. If he puts his hands on her, I'll…"

"I don't like this anymore than you. Why are you so upset? She's my daughter."

CHAPTER SEVEN

Answers

Dylan drove to the lake and parked near a stretch of beach. Given the time of year, the shore would be deserted. They'd have the solitude they needed to talk unencumbered. For an extended moment, they sat in silence, enjoying the tranquility. It had been a difficult day; the seclusion was a welcomed relief.

The moonlight reflected off the water and provided the only illumination. However, Chrissie could see for miles off the bay. She preferred darkness to sunlight. Once she settled down, she closed her eyes and leaned against the headrest. Serenity washed over her and erased the stress of the last few hours.

Without warning, Dylan disrupted the stillness. "I thought we came here to talk."

Unnerved by the unexpected interruption, she turned and glared at him. "We did." Her apprehension soared; she dreaded this unavoidable discussion. Chrissie wanted to solve this conundrum but feared what she might learn.

Dylan must have understood her distress. He reached out and caressed her hand. "We don't need to talk now if you don't want to. It's up to you."

His smoldering eyes burned as he lifted her chin with his finger. The touch of his hand sent chills through her body, and a tingle ran up her spine. Their faces now inches apart, an intoxicating aroma of apple-cinnamon embraced her nostrils. His warm breath encircled her countenance.

Chrissie struggled to clear her mind, as she needed to concentrate on the issue at hand. The task proved mammoth, and Dylan's allure melted her resistance. Excited by his proximity, she knew she must compose herself. She turned her head to break his mesmerizing gaze. Then, she took a deep breath, and forced herself to speak. "We need to talk."

Dylan smiled, his playful air returning. "Ask me any question. What do you want to know?" Did he realize her predicament and want to give her a graceful way out?

"I know you're something other than human." Chrissie felt a little foolish when she babbled, "But I don't know what you are."

He snickered. "That's not a question; that's a comment."

Frustrated, Chrissie sighed. "You know what I mean, Dylan. What are you?"

Dylan teased, "Hmm. I could tell you, but then I'd have to kill you." He laughed at his own joke.

Sometimes, his endless banter proved annoying. "So, why did you bring me out here, if you're not going to tell me the truth?" she complained. His humor did not amuse her in the least.

Dylan took her face in his hand and stared into her eyes. "Are you sure you want to know what I am? It may not be pretty."

More than wanting, she needed to know the truth. She had invested too much in this puzzle. It must be solved. "I don't care. I need to know." Dylan clenched his jaws and said nothing for several minutes. When Chrissie could stand the silence no longer, she exhaled and focused her gaze on the floor mat. "Dylan, do you know what I am?"

As though it was the norm, he stated, "Yes, I know exactly what you are. You're a vampire."

"If you know what I am, then shouldn't I know what you are? It isn't as though I'm going to tell anyone your secret." More than ever, she wanted as much knowledge of him as he had about her. Although they had known each other for a short time, there was already an emotional attachment. She longed to know more.

"I get that." He bit the inside of his lip and groaned. "I'm a drachmon."

Chrissie's jaw dropped. She stared at him before she blurted in astonishment. "A what?" In disbelief, she frowned. "What's a drachmon?" Did she look as stupid as she felt?

Turning his head, he faced the windshield. "We are creatures of legend, as you are."

"So, that's why your presence doesn't bother me. When I told my father you don't make me thirsty, he demanded to see you."

"Why was he so concerned?"

"Because it isn't natural," she explained. "Although we can control our thirst in the company of humans, the smell of their blood causes our salivary glands to water."

"My blood is different from a human's."

"Yeah, I gathered that." She spoke nervously. "I've never heard of a drachmon."

"That's because we stay out of the spotlight. Unlike vampires, we live in a world of secrecy."

"What do you mean? Vampires don't advertise themselves." Chrissie felt the need to defend her species.

"Really." He sneered. "Then why are there so many movies, TV shows, and books about your species?" His disdain was obvious.

"That's just human imagination. Most of what they portray is myth. We don't have anything to do with that."

"Christina." A shiver surprised her when Dylan said her name. "Have you ever stopped to think that someone is feeding the myth to them?"

She blinked, then cleared her throat to regain her composure. "No vampire would set out to expose himself knowing the repercussions."

"Really, are you sure about that?" He smirked.

"I don't want to argue about it. Let's say you're right. What does that have to do with the question of who you are?"

"I'll explain the connection." He paused. "I descended from what mythology calls a dragon."

Bewildered, Chrissie exclaimed, "What? I thought dragons were lizard-like creatures that breathed fire."

Dylan contorted his face as he disclosed facts of his heritage. "Like so many other human fallacies, the stories of dragons are erroneous. Dragons weren't lizard-like creatures. They looked more like men with wings. However, for centuries they did commit despicable acts."

Confused, Chrissie shook her head. "I don't get it. You said they, but you also said you were a dragon."

"You didn't let me finish. I'm not a dragon. I'm a drachmon. There's a difference." He hesitated before he continued. The suspense had her on edge. "My ancestors were brutal savages. They raided villages, tortured and killed men for sport, then captured their women and girls for breeding. You see, very few females are born to us, so sometimes we take mates from outside our species."

"Is that why you're here, to find a mate?"

"No, not really. If I find one, good, but that's not my primary motivation." He stared out the window. "If I find a human female I cared about, I wouldn't condemn her to certain death."

"I don't understand what you mean."

Recounting his ancestral horrors exacted a heavy toll on him. Chrissie wished she could somehow ease his pain, but there was nothing she could do. He gazed up at the stars before he sighed and continued, "Most breeding attempts with humans were unsuccessful. There were no offspring. About one in a hundred produced a live birth, and those offspring were flawed. Even if a human female were impregnated, the child would kill her long before full gestation. If, by some miracle she was able to carry a child long enough for it to survive outside the womb, she'd become its first meal." He tapped his incisors. "We are born hungry, with a full set of razor sharp teeth."

Although Chrissie empathized with him, her curiosity got the better of her. "I still don't understand where you're going with this."

He put his finger on her lip to silence her. "If you keep interrupting me, Christina, I'll never be able to finish."

A resurgence of the tingling sensation spiraled down Chrissie's spine. She trembled, but managed enough control to retain her poise. "I'm sorry. I'll be quiet and listen."

"Legend says," he continued, "that one day, a beautiful female with strange supernatural powers was captured and imprisoned in the tribal village. She captivated the hearts of many males, and several warriors lost their lives fighting to possess her. Among my clan, it is believed that she was a witch.

Her powers proved so useful that the ruling council issued an edict that she was not to be touched. Elonda, a tribal warrior, found her beauty irresistible. One night while she slept, he crept into her chamber and forced himself upon her. As a result of his attack, she became pregnant. The delivery was difficult, but by some miracle, she survived the birth of twin boys.

Enraged by all she had endured, she plotted her revenge. One day, when she was left unguarded, she made her way out of the village and escaped with her children. For ten years, she nursed her hatred. When she returned, she brought an army of creatures far more powerful than anything else the dragons had ever encountered, vampires. In retribution, she and her forces destroyed the entire clan. Only her offspring remained as evidence of their existence. Not even her children escaped her wrath. As punishment for their father's misdeeds, the twins and all their descendants inherited the responsibility of protecting the balance between the natural and the supernatural world, only interfering when the balance of power shifted."

"Humph, the sour grapes eaten by the father set the children's teeth on edge."

Dylan glanced over at her sullenly. "Something like that."

Chrissie slanted her head to one side. "Are you saying you're one of the twins?"

He closed his eyes as though he were trying to shut out the memories. "No." Sadness echoed in his voice. "I'm one of her descendants."

Unsure of how to react to this incredible narrative, Chrissie sat in silence for a moment, brushing her cheek with her fingertips. "So you're saying your job is to protect humans from vampires."

Dylan shook his head "No. A certain number of deaths is expected. After all, we all survive off the death of something, even vegetarians." A humorless smile grazed his lips. "Our job is to ensure supernatural beings don't declare open season on humans."

Knowing her worries had been unwarranted, Chrissie felt a sense of relief wash over her. She hoped this information would alleviate her father's concerns as well. "That doesn't sound so bad. You had me nervous for a minute there."

A pained expression haunted Dylan's face. "Don't you understand what that means, Christina?" He waited for several seconds. When Chrissie did not respond, he confessed, "I've killed vampires."

Chrissie turned to face him. "I suspected as much." She scrutinized the side of his face before she added, "I'm sure you had your reasons. It wasn't for sport, was it?"

Dylan leaned his head back on the headrest. "I've told you, anytime humans are threatened with wholesale carnage, we step in." He peeked at her. "It's what we do. It isn't just vampires. It's any creature that threatens their existence."

"If that's true, why is it I've never heard anything about your species? Professor Marshall and my dad didn't seem to know anything about you either."

"We're cautious." He nodded his head. "Those who come into contact with us don't survive to tell the tale."

As she processed his disclosure, Chrissie blinked numerous times. Her inquisitiveness aroused, she inquired, "How many of you are there?"

The muscles in Dylan's chest expanded. "Our numbers are few, about six thousand warriors to guard the world's population." He winked at her. "We don't need a large number. We're lethal."

Fearing his answer, Chrissie half joked. "So, you're saying if you had to, you would destroy me."

Like a soldier called to attention, he leaned forward. "Don't even joke about that. I would never, ever, hurt you or your dad."

Caught off guard by the force of his answer, she flinched. Then her temper flared. "You seemed willing to hurt him tonight." She didn't like being chastised.

His muscles relaxed. With a roguish grin, he snickered. "I wouldn't have killed him. I might have hurt him a little." A sparkle danced in his eyes. "After all, he's a vampire. It isn't like he wouldn't heal."

Chrissie couldn't decide whether to take him seriously or not. Still, his boyish charm worked its magic again. She chuckled. "What about Professor Marshall?"

Dylan sat back. He smacked his lips, exposing his razors. "I told you. We're meat eaters, and we're born hungry. The professor's old hide might be a little tough." A mischievous air lightened his features. "But, I could manage to get him down." Amused by his rather convoluted joke, he whooped. "Although, I'll bet he would give me indigestion."

She chortled. "You're incorrigible."

Rolling his eyes playfully, Dylan crowed, "I know."

Though Chrissie enjoyed his wisecracks, she bit her lip to restrain her mirth. "May I ask you another question? It has nothing to do with what you are."

He sighed. "What do you want to know?"

"Well." She wriggled in her seat to make herself comfortable. "Why do you attend school with humans?"

Leaning his head against the headrest, he fixed his eyes on the top of the car. "Good question." He seemed to speak more to himself than to Chrissie. "I wanted to know what they were like. I heard they were selfish, self-center beings with no redeeming quality. I had never spent a significant amount of time with them, so I wanted to see for myself."

She propped her arm against the seat, her fist under her chin. "Do you agree with those opinions?"

"Some of them, but not all. What do you think of them?"

Chrissie mulled over her answer. "I don't know. Of course, I don't see things the same way anymore. When I was human, there were several people who impressed me as honorable—my grandmother for instance. She was wonderful. I depended on her for everything." She smiled at the memory of her nana. No one had ever been as close to Chrissie as she had been. "She never let me down." Of course, she loved her dad, but Nana had nurtured her during the tender years of her childhood. This relationship created an unbreakable bond between them. "I will admit; however, this is my first experience being around humans since my transformation."

"Really." He gazed at her. "Where were you for all that time?"

"We lived on a ranch in Arizona for seven years — thirty miles from the nearest town."

"Why?"

"I needed seclusion. You see, I had to master my thirst before I could interact with humans. Dad says I still have a long way to go. He's always harping on me about honing my skills." She flexed her fingers. "Anyway, he decided the time was right for me to attend school, so here I am." She paused to wait for a response. Dylan didn't react, so she added, "You said you came here to learn about humans. Where were you?"

"I remained in my village for most of my life. When I decided I wanted to be on my own, I came here. My first experience with humans was in the 90's. I started college..." An unreadable shadow fell over his countenance. "I didn't return after the first year."

Chrissie turned to the windshield. She thought she understood his unspoken truth. "You said you're a warrior." Glaring at the moon, she asked, "What happens if you're needed?"

"They send for me, and I go."

"How do they get word to you?"

"We have our ways." Dylan glanced at his watch. Just as she opened her mouth to ask the location of his village, he interrupted her. "It's getting late. I should get you home. Your father is probably ready to send in the militia by now."

Chrissie stuck out her lower lip. "I'm not ready to go home." She didn't want the evening to end. However, in the split second it took to process the situation, she realized he was right. "I hadn't thought of that. My dad will be worried sick if I stay away much longer."

Dylan positioned his immense hand atop hers. Goose bumps erupted on her arms. "I don't want to go either, but we have tomorrow."

Anxious to see him again, even before they parted, Chrissie beamed a wide grin. "What time do you have class tomorrow?"

Dylan roared with laughter.

Embarrassed, Chrissie attempted to snatch her hand from his grasp. But, he was stronger than she'd imagined. Were vampires really the strongest creatures in the universe? She would have to reconsider the belief. "*How conceited of me.*"

Still grinning, Dylan shook his head. He pulled her hand to his lips. As he kissed her palm, he answered, "My first class is at ten. I'll finish at eleven." He sandwiched her small hands between his. "If you don't mind, I'll drop by your house afterwards."

Chrissie grumbled, "I've changed my mind. I don't think I want to see you tomorrow."

Dylan kissed her hand again. Without taking his eyes off her, he traced the contours of her lips with the tip of his finger. Butterflies fluttered in her stomach, causing her spine to quiver. He leaned in close to her ear. "You know, a lesser man would be intimidated by that explosive temper of yours." His sweet breath spiraled into her nostrils.

With defenses stripped, Chrissie struggled to maintain self-control. She focused on his chest. "Then it's good you're not a lesser man."

Dylan's voice echoed his sincerity. "Can I see you tomorrow?"

His serious demeanor captivated her. She lifted her gaze to meet his. "I'll be home until four-thirty. You can stop by any time."

"Awesome. I'll see you tomorrow around noon." He hedged before he continued. "I'm curious about something."

"What?"

"I always thought vampires were destroyed by the sunlight. You come to class before dark. Why?"

Now, it was her turn to laugh. "We're allergic to strong sunlight. We avoid the sun during midday, but mornings and late afternoons are fine."

Dylan frowned. "What happens to you?"

"Have you ever wondered why vampires can exist when their hearts don't beat?"

"I've never given it much thought. Until I met you, vampires were just problems to be dealt with when the need arose."

She flinched. "Well anyway, vampires are like sponges. Our bodies absorb fluids. That's why our internal organs work without a heartbeat."

He raised a brow. "Your internal organs work?" He sounded astonished.

"Of course they work. Haven't you noticed I breathe? Something has to be working. Be logical."

"Why doesn't your heart work?"

Chrissie cleared her throat. "It's like the appendix in humans. It's there, but we don't need it."

"So what does that have to do with your being allergic to the sun?"

"Allergic is the wrong word." She scratched her head, then smoothed her ruffled locks. "Like a sponge, the sun depletes our moisture. The hotter the sun, the more blood we need to consume." She shrugged. "So we avoid it."

Dylan draped his arm over the steering wheel. "So if you stayed in the sun too long what would happen?"

"Let's just say, you wouldn't want me around a human."

"Wow!"

"Aren't you repulsed?"

"Not really."

Chrissie ran her fingers over the dashboard. "Can I ask one more question?"

"Nope."

"Please. It's a simple one."

Dylan drew in a deep breath and exhaled. "Okay, what is it?"

"How old are you?"

Facing the windshield, he asked, "Why?"

"I'm just curious."

He muttered. "I, I'm forty-six."

Chrissie stretched her neck to scrutinize his features. "You don't look a day over nineteen."

"Thanks."

"But why?"

"Why what?

She sighed. "Why do you look so young?"

"My people age slower than most species. My mother is over a hundred and fifty, and she looks around twenty. None of my species looks more than thirty." He tapped the end of her nose. "Since we're on the subject of age, don't tell anyone else you're twenty-five."

Chrissie sat up straight. "Why not?"

"Because you don't look any older than seventeen — eighteen at the most. What will you do ten years from now when you're thirty-five?" He turned up his nose. "Your father should have told you that."

Fingertip in her mouth, she bit the nail. "He did." With a frown etched across her forehead, she confessed, "When you asked me, the truth just spilled out."

Dylan glared at her. "You need to be careful with that, Christina. One slip could give you away."

She smirked. Her father called her *Christina* when he was angry. "I know. I will. I'm curious about something else though." She hedged before she asked, "How long does your species live?"

"I don't know of anyone who died of natural causes. The only deaths I know of happened in battle."

"So you can die."

"Yeah. We can die. It's rare though. Remember. I told you about my dad. "

She gasped. "That's why you didn't believe your stepfather. Because he said your father, just died."

"Yeah. We don't *just die*." Chrissie could hear the bitterness in his voice. "Our heads have to be severed or our hearts must be damaged beyond regeneration." Abruptly, he started the ignition. "I've got to get you home before your father sends a posse after me."

Chrissie smiled. Her father wouldn't need a posse. He'd charge in like the Lone Ranger with Professor Marshall tagging along as Tonto. She mused. *"Why does Professor Marshall seem so interested in what I do?"*

* * * * *

Dylan pulled onto the long snakelike drive that led to Chrissie's home. She visualized her father in his den frantic with worry. In her mind's eye, she pictured him pacing in front of the window that overlooked the forest below. The confrontation she feared loomed on the horizon, filling her with dread. Her willful disobedience toward her father would no doubt have infuriated him.

Once they parked, Chrissie glanced at the digital clock on the dash. She wanted to gauge whether she'd face a thunderstorm or a tornado. They arrived at ten minutes to three — definitely a tornado. She grabbed the door handle. "Well, goodnight."

Dylan reached for her hand. "You don't need to go in right this minute if you don't want to. We can sit here for a while if you'd like."

Goosebumps erupted down the length of her arm. She swallowed hard to force herself to concentrate. "No, I'd better go. Dad can hear our conversation." She stared at the floor. "I don't think it would be wise to push him any further tonight." When a muffled growl floated from William's den, she bit the side of her jaw.

"You're right." Dylan kissed Chrissie's palm. "We've caused enough confusion for one night." Aware William could hear him, Dylan released her hand and faced the house. "Professor Garrett, I'm sorry about the misunderstanding this evening. Chrissie will explain everything. I hope afterwards we can put this to rest. I really like Chrissie. I would hate to lose her friendship." The growling inside the house intensified.

At that moment, Chrissie understood why she felt so enamored with Dylan. She could tell his apology was heartfelt. Because of his sincerity, her feelings for him deepened. No other man would have apologized with her father within striking distance of him.

In appreciation of his magnanimous gesture, she mouthed, "Thank you."

Dylan smiled and winked at her. Chrissie pulled the door's latch, but he maintained a grip on her hand. When she turned back toward him, his face, now inches away, descended until his lips pressed against hers. The kiss began tenderly, but increased in its intensity. Sparks raged throughout her body. Her entire being ignited into a towering inferno, leaving her smoldering with delight. Though her intellect had been the pride of her existence, under Dylan's touch, it dissolved into a burned out cinder. Realizing her father could hear everything, she tried not to make a sound. However, controlling her passion proved impossible.

With his eyes shut, Dylan ended the kiss. His heart pounded like the proverbial hammer. He pulled Chrissie to his chest and held her locked in his embrace, his face resting against her forehead. A deep guttural sigh escaped from his full lips. Barely able to break the invisible chain that bound him, he pulled away. "You'd better go in."

Unexpected passion caused Chrissie's body to shiver as she struggled to gain control. While she yearned to linger in his arms, her reasoning had returned. The need to face her father hovered in her mind. Before she extricated herself, she leaned in to kiss his neck. The heat from his body surrounded her. This time it was he who trembled at her touch. Turning to leave her fantasy behind, she murmured, "Goodnight, Dylan."

* * * * *

When Chrissie stepped in the foyer, the darkness engulfed her. Apprehension seized her heart. Despite the fact that she could see the smallest details with clarity, the shadows created a sense of inescapable doom. With great dexterity, she tiptoed down the hall and peeped to the left into the living room. Driven by the necessity to unwind before she faced the inevitable, she stepped into the spacious area. She strolled to the French doors to admire the beauty of the garden below. Across the room, the white Tux loveseat, situated in the alcove, beckoned her. When she reached the cozy couch, she sat down. Its depth enfolded her, providing a much needed safe haven.

As she lounged in the comfortable atmosphere of her personal sanctuary, she heard her father rise from his overstuffed chair in his den. With a deep breath, she prepared herself for the onslaught of emotions she knew she would face. To her surprise, William headed toward the backstairs.

Concerned she had inflicted such immense pain on her dad he didn't even want to talk to her, she panicked. "What's wrong, Daddy?"

William's footsteps grew dimmer as he ascended the stairs. "I don't want to talk tonight, Christina. We'll talk in the morning."

Though she couldn't see him, Chrissie stood and faced the direction of the staircase. "Would you like to sit with me in the living room? We don't need to talk." Her concern grew exponentially. As her dad climbed the steps, she wondered if their relationship would ever recover.

William meandered along the hallway to his room. When he stood before the door, he answered, "Not tonight, Christina."

Chrissie closed her eyes. *"Two consecutive Christina's, he must be furious."*

"I need to think." He didn't sound angry. On the contrary, he sounded defeated.

Chrissie looked up at the ceiling. "Daddy, are you okay?" Sticking her fingernail between her front teeth, she asked, "Are you really, really mad at me?" Her spirits sank as she heard William shut his door. She could stand his anger, but not his rejection. For eighteen years she'd waited for a father. Having someone to call Dad had been incredible. Her mind spinning, she sat on the couch. *"How could I have risked losing such a precious relationship?"*

As William eased into his chair, Chrissie heard the leather creak. "I'm not angry with you. I just don't want to have this discussion until I've had an opportunity to evaluate the situation from all angles." His spoke with cold, hard logic. "We've had enough harsh words tonight. I don't want either of us to say anything else we'll regret."

Devastated by his detached attitude, Chrissie regretted her callous remarks to him. Had she lost the love of the one man who had ever mattered to her — that is until now? Pressing to break the ice, she persisted. "Daddy, can we talk?"

"Not tonight, Christina."

Chrissie squeezed her eyes shut. *"Christina again. What happened to Chrissie or Peanut?"* She opened her eyes and peered at the ceiling. "What are you going to do?"

The ice in William's tone chilled the room. "I'm going to read."

Loneliness crept in on Chrissie. She missed the camaraderie with her dad. She missed Dylan, and she felt abandoned. *"Wow, what a difference a day makes."*

Since she had nothing else to occupy her mind, Chrissie decided to read a novel. She wandered into her father's den to scan his vast collection. Though William had representations from several genres, nothing in particular caught her eye. Frustrated, she grabbed the selection closest to her and headed for her room. She spent the next thirty minutes sprawled across her bed, flipping through pages. When the clock in the foyer struck four, she realized she didn't remember a thing she had read. She sighed and tossed the book on the floor.

Chrissie glanced at her cell phone on the nightstand. A part of her hoped Dylan would call, but it was better that he didn't. She still hadn't talked to her dad.

Time dragged by. As the sun peeked over the horizon, she crawled out of bed to watch the sunrise. She massaged her forehead. *"I thought this night would never end?"*

As though he could hear her thoughts, her father called out." "Christina, would you meet me in the den?"

The sense of disaster she'd felt the night before had vanished. She found herself looking forward to a discussion with her father. Happy to reconnect with her dad, she took the backstairs two steps at a time. When she reached the room, William was sitting behind his glossy oak desk. He greeted her with a smile. "Come in, and have a seat."

Chrissie sat in the chair directly in front of the desk. Suspicion flooded her mind. *"Why the relaxed attitude? What has changed in the preceding four hours?"* Cautious, she asked, "Are you ready to talk?"

He leaned back in his seat. His elbows rested on the arms. "As a matter-of-fact, I am. I've had time to consider our confrontation." He sat up straight. "I've decided we were both to blame. I, for reacting to Walter's accusations without corroborating evidence, and *you* for defying me."

Not wanting any misunderstanding, she interrupted, "I'm sorry I defied you, Dad, but I had a very good reason. Dylan explained everything to me. When you hear the story, I think it will put your mind at ease about him."

"I'll try to listen objectively to your explanation. However, I warn you I'm not feeling generous where that young man is concerned."

"If you promise to listen with an open mind, that's all I'll ask."

"I promise I'll try."

Chrissie related Dylan's narrative, striving not to omit any of the pertinent details, yet careful not to reveal too much. William frowned and tapped the end of his nose with his index finger, a habit he performed when he doubted her veracity.

When she had finished her account of the facts, he began the inquisition. He put the tips of his two index fingers together and pressed them against his closed lips. "So, you're saying that he, and his kind ensure that the balance between the natural, and the supernatural remains at a constant."

She scowled. A small spark of anger ignited within her. The idea of her father talking about her—her what—like that, didn't set well with her. "I'm not comfortable with your referring to Dylan's people as, *his kind.*"

William propped his elbows on the desk. "According to you, he's not a person." He rested his chin on his cupped hands. "In fairness, let's say his species then."

In an effort to take advantage of his blunder, Chrissie asked, "Dad, are you trying to provoke me?" If she stalled long enough, it might prevent him from asking the questions she dreaded.

Seemingly unfazed by her comments, he continued. "I'm asking questions because I'm trying to understand." His face hardened. "If, indeed, it is his job to protect mankind, I want to know what that means." The frown in his forehead deepened. "How does he accomplish it?"

Chrissie knew she wouldn't be able to avoid his question. Attempting to evade his gaze, she focused on the books atop his desk — all of which dealt with the attainment of wealth. William wanted to know as much as he could about money. That's why he became a professor of economics, and it was paying off. He had amassed a small fortune. *"What strange thoughts to have during such a serious conversation."* For a split second, she considered lying. She dismissed the thought. Her father needed to know the truth. How much information should she reveal? Nervously, she cleared her throat. "Well. Uh. From what I understand, sometimes, he and the other warriors in his village are forced to eliminate the threat."

Resting his elbow on the arm of his chair, William stroked his mustache. His fangs protruded just enough to be visible. "Eliminate the threat. What you're trying to avoid telling me, is that he kills vampires."

Chrissie flinched at the blaze in his eyes. "If he's forced to, but it isn't just vampires. Dylan kills any beings that threaten humanity with excessive carnage. He understands there will always be some deaths. His goal involves the prevention of unnecessary slaughter." She didn't mention that his ancestors had once hunted humans for sport.

"You said his village of warriors. How many of these warriors are there?"

She frowned. *"Why is the exact number important?"* Although she didn't understand his motive for asking, she told the truth. "Only about six thousand."

William stared straight ahead, unblinking, unresponsive. Chrissie fixed her eyes on the crevices hardening in his face. She waited for him to say something. As fretfulness swept over her, she battled an impulse to scream. Unable to stand the silence, she broke the ice. "Dad, what's wrong?"

He stayed silent, arms folded across his chest, eyes narrowed, muscles tensed, pensive. Suddenly, he blinked. Then he looked at her as though he just had an epiphany. "So. How do you feel about him now that you have this information?" William's tone echoed his uneasiness.

Chrissie arched her body forward. "I, I still like him," she stammered, "a lot." She bit down on her bottom lip. "I think he likes me too. We're planning to see each other on a regular basis."

William shook his head in frustration. "I don't understand your reasoning, Christina. How could you still want to see this young man?" His disapproval resonated in each word.

Chrissie's temper reared its ugly head. She leapt from her seat, coiled, ready to strike. "You don't even know him," she protested. "You're jumping to conclusions. I think you're a bigot."

Sometimes, she was a little too honest for her own good. Her nana always said, *"If you don't want to know the truth, don't ask Chrissie."* This was one of those moments when being a good liar would have been an asset, "Que Sera, Sera."

Like a tightly wound spring, William popped up. He slammed his fist against the desk. "How dare you call me that? I am not a bigot. I'm thinking about your welfare, young lady. You don't know this young man. Yet, you want me to say it's alright for you to date him. You don't have a clue what he is capable of doing."

His intensity caught Chrissie off guard, and she blanched. The seconds it took for her to retreat afforded her enough time to process all that had been said. In an effort to alleviate the tension, she relented. "I hadn't thought about it like that. I'm sorry about what I said. I was just angry."

"I loved your mother more than you will ever know. Her race didn't matter to me. She could have been green, and I wouldn't have cared. The only reason we kept our relationship a secret was because she feared her parents' reaction."

"I'm so sorry, Daddy. I know how much you and Mom loved each other."

The veins in William's temples relaxed. "Would it do any good to ask you not to see him?"

Chrissie eased into her seat. "We're planning to see each other today. As a matter-of-fact, he's coming by the house after his 10:00 o'clock class. We're going to spend time here, before I go to school."

"I'm not comfortable with your seeing this young man." William sat down as well. "He makes me very nervous."

"I understand you're concerned about me." She rose and walked to his side of the desk. "You can't shield me from life, no matter how much you love me. I'm a *grown woman*."

William shook his head. "No, baby. You don't know men. You haven't been around them. I stole that chance from you when you were eighteen."

Taking his hand in hers, Chrissie leaned against the desk. "Daddy. I'm not overly experienced, but I know what I feel. I've lived in an emotional abyss all my life. I don't want to be alone anymore." She placed her forehead against his. "Whatever destiny holds for me, I'll face it. I've started this journey into daylight with Dylan, and I need to finish it."

The corners of William's mouth turned up. "Since when did you get so smart?"

Feeble as it was, Chrissie knew she had won when she saw the smile. He may not have approved, but he would no longer fight her.

CHAPTER EIGHT

Courtship

Chrissie sat in English half listening to Mrs. Phillips. She had read and researched *Troilus and Cressida* and the lecture seemed pointless to her. Shoving her hands into the pocket of her hoodie, she texted Estefina. "I will never understand why professors ask you to read a book if they're going to lecture you about the obvious."

Estefina, who sat in the desk next to Chrissie, glanced at the phone atop her desk. She answered, "LOL! This is killing me. Glad you're here."

With the phone just far enough out of her pocket to read the text, Chrissie set her nimble fingers into motion. "Why? Because misery loves company. LOL."

As soon as Chrissie hit the send button, Mrs. Phillips strolled by her desk. "Miss Garrett, I know you're texting. If you're not interested in the lecture, please leave."

Chrissie glanced up sheepishly. "I'm sorry. I won't do it again."

To reinforce her objection, Mrs. Phillips scowled. "See to it that you don't."

With their conversation quashed, the hour dragged by. When class ended, Chrissie and Estefina gathered their books and stuffed them into their backpacks. Chrissie shuddered. "I'm past ready to get out of here."

Headed toward the door, Estefina asked, "Would you like to go hang out at the Shack?" Some of the guys are meeting there tonight."

"Any other time, I'd love to go, but I'm meeting Dylan. We're going to a movie."

Estefina pushed the door open. "Have you been seeing a lot of him?" She smiled. "I think he likes you. He treats you with more respect than the other girls."

Chrissie focused on the floor. Though she felt somewhat awkward, she longed to hear more. "What do you mean by that?" It pleased her that someone else had noticed he treated her special.

"I can't explain it." Estefina shrugged. "I can tell you're special to him just by the way he looks at you."

As the duo stepped through the ornate double doors of Jefferson Hall, Chrissie spotted Dylan. His black baseball cap turned backwards, he stood leaning against her car with his massive arms folded. His eyes locked on hers the moment she crossed the threshold of the building. At first, he flashed a gorgeous grin. Then, his face contorted into a frown as he glared at Chrissie's head. "Hi."

Chrissie ran her fingers through her silken strands. The way he stared at her made her feel self-conscious. "What's wrong?"

His nose wriggled as though he smelled something foul. "What happened to your hair?"

Rubbing the back of her crown with her palm, Chrissie asked, "What do you mean?"

"Why is your hair straight?"

Tight-lipped, Chrissie mumbled, "I flat ironed it. I like to wear it straight sometimes."

Dylan sifted her silky locks through his fingers, and then watched them fall back into place. "I don't like it. You have beautiful, curly hair. Why would you ruin it by flat ironing it?"

She pushed out her bottom lip. "I like variety sometimes, Dylan. You should try it."

He shrugged. "Just saying." He turned to Estefina for confirmation. "Do you like her hair this way, or do you like it better curly. Be honest."

Estefina turned and bolted away. As she executed her escape, she shouted back. "I'm not getting in that. I'll see you tomorrow, Chrissie."

"See you." Chrissie watched Estefina leave, aware that Dylan had never altered his gaze. Like all humans, Estefina's blood made her salivate, but she had learned to control her urges. Their friendship was more important than a momentary indulgence.

Once Estefina turned the corner, Dylan grabbed Chrissie's backpack. "What do you want to do tonight?"

Relieved that he had changed the subject, she grinned. "I thought we were going to a movie."

He slung her backpack over his shoulder. "I don't want to go to a movie."

"Well, I don't care what we do."

The couple meandered toward Chrissie's car. "I have an outstanding idea." He winked at her. "Let's go hang out at your house."

This time, she ogled him in disbelief. "You're kidding, right."

"Nope."

"Why in the world would you want to hang out at my house?" She seriously questioned his sanity. "My dad will be home tonight."

"There's no time like the present for your dad to get used to seeing me around. Anyway, it'll give us a chance to get to know each other better."

"By us, do you mean you and me, or you and Dad?"

When they reached the car, Dylan set the backpack on the hood. Pulling Chrissie to him, he leaned against the side of the vehicle. "Why, me and your father, of course. I intend for him to think of me like a son before it's over."

With raised brows, Chrissie rested the palm of her hands against his chest. "You're sick. You know that, right?" She didn't find his twisted humor the least bit funny.

Dylan put his finger on her lips. "Everybody loves me. Why shouldn't your father?"

"I am aware of that, Dylan. Thank you." She traced the length of his leather jacket with her fingertips. His self-assurance never ceased to amaze her. "Are you sure you want to press for this particular relationship right now?"

He elevated her chin. "Why not?"

"Because my father isn't exactly your biggest fan."

Dylan grinned. "Give him time. He will be."

Chrissie wondered if he had forgotten how close he had come to all out war three weeks before. Though he visited her the day following his confrontation with her dad, she had been home alone. The intervening weeks hadn't changed her father's opinion. Nonetheless, she acquiesced. "Alright, but be careful what you ask for."

Dylan opened the door for Chrissie. "Do you want me to follow you, or do you want to ride with me?" He tossed her backpack into the passenger's seat. "I'll bring you back later to pick up your car."

Chrissie sat in the driver's seat. "I'll drive my car home." He shut the door. "There's no sense in you making two trips."

* * * * *

Chrissie parked in her usual spot in the garage, and Dylan parked his truck directly behind her. When Chrissie exited her car, she sauntered to his window. "Why don't you park inside the garage?"

With a delighted pull of the lips, he teased, "No thanks. I may need to make a quick getaway."

"Ha, ha, very funny," Chrissie mocked, "if you're so afraid, why did you insist we come?"

Dylan said nothing. He got out of his truck and strolled up to her. Then, he put his arms around her waist, pulling her close. "I really like you." Dylan searched her eyes. "I do want to make a good impression on your father. I can tell how much you love him. So, I want him to like me."

Chrissie rested her head on his chest. The sincerity of his words caught her off guard. She could always see through his façade. This kind of openness tore at the emotional walls feeling abandoned had constructed. The loss of her mother at a young age, and the lack of a father for eighteen years, had caused the fortress around her heart. Other than her dad and her nana, Chrissie allowed no one to penetrate her fortification. Now, Dylan had pierced her defenses. She felt as though she had known, and loved him all her life. Inside his jacket, she snuggled her arms. *"I wonder if this is what people refer to as a soul mate. Only time will tell."* His touch always made her quiver, and this was no exception. Closing her eyes, she breathed in his essence. "Let's go inside."

The couple entered the house through the garage door, which led into the kitchen. It was an enormous room with modern, energy efficient appliances. Other than the refrigerator to store blood, they never used anything; the microwave was used to warm it.

Dylan's eyes zeroed in on the refrigerator. "What have you got to eat?" He opened the door to search the contents.

"We don't have anything you'd find appetizing. Sorry." It was rather embarrassing to have nothing but containers of blood in the frig.

"It's okay." He closed the refrigerator. "I'm not that hungry anyway. I'll grab something when I leave."

She rested her palms on the counter. "Tomorrow I'll go to the grocery store. What kind of foods do you like?"

"I'm a meat eater. Any kind of red meat will do." He joined her by the sink. "When it's available, I prefer wild game."

"I don't know how to prepare it. I wasn't good in the kitchen when I was mortal. Now, there's no need for it."

"I'd rather have it raw, anyway." He tapped his razor sharp teeth. "I thought all human females honed their domestic skills in hopes of snagging a husband."

"Even when I was human, I wasn't your typical female. I found books and sports far more interesting than boys."

As they talked, Chrissie led the way from the kitchen through the dining area, then down the stairs into the family room. The black leather couch, loveseat, and matching chair arranged in a horseshoe pattern complemented the light blue walls. The dark hues enhanced the cozy feel of the room. She turned on the sixty inch flat screen television. The duo sat on the couch together. "What would you like to watch?"

"I'd like to watch the news." He winked. "I like to keep up with what's going on in the world."

She flipped through the channels until she came to CNN. "Are you interested in something in particular?"

"No, we can watch something else if you prefer."

"That's okay. I was just curious." She placed the remote on the coffee table.

"I'm curious about something, too. How do you manage to have so much human blood in your refrigerator?"

"Dad has a friend at a blood bank. He keeps us supplied."

"You mean you have a human who brings you blood." His astonishment resonated in his inflection.

"Yes."

Stretching his arms across the back of the sofa, Dylan asked, "Why does he do it? What's in it for him?"

Chrissie scratched the back of her head and then smoothed the ruffled hair. "Well. Friend isn't an accurate description of their relationship. In truth, Joshua is my father's familiar. Dad met Josh years ago when he was first turned. He hadn't developed any self-control, and he bit him."

"How does that work." He leaned forward to focus on her face. "I know that if a vampire bites a human, they develop a loyalty to them. I don't understand why."

Before she answered, Chrissie pushed the cuticle of her index finger back with her thumb nail. She hoped the knowledge would not repulse him. "When a vampire bites a person, if he doesn't die, he becomes a part of the vampire forever."

He canted his head to one side in reflection. "I still don't understand how it works."

"It's like a virus without a cure. The infection spreads throughout the body. An individual may not seem to have any symptoms at a given moment, but the virus remains in his body."

Expressionless, Dylan dug deeper. "How is it manifested?" He didn't appear repelled by her explanation. On the contrary, he seemed quite impressed.

Given his reaction, Chrissie felt a bit more inclined to divulge the particulars. "To a degree, we can control a person's will. It resembles hypnotism. We can't make someone do anything that goes contrary to his basic nature, but we can manipulate them if it's something they're capable of doing, anyway."

"So. Do you have a familiar?"

Chrissie tucked her bottom lip under her front teeth and squeezed her eyes. When she opened them, Dylan's gaze was fixed on her face. She swallowed hard. "Yes."

Dylan rose. With his back to her, he strolled to the fireplace. When he turned, he asked for the information she didn't want to reveal. "Is it a man or a woman?"

Through expanded cheeks, Chrissie exhaled. "It's a man."

"Is he in love with you?"

As she joined him at the hearth, Chrissie asked, "What kind of question is that?"

"It's a question that I want to know the answer to." Dylan gripped the mantel with such force Chrissie thought it would break. "Now, answer it. Is he in love with you?" There was no humor in his expression, only anger.

Wide-eyed, Chrissie eased close to him. "What would make you think that?" It startled her that Dylan reacted with such intensity so soon in their relationship.

He stepped away from her. "You're avoiding the question."

Chrissie stammered. "I, I suppose. I hadn't thought about it one way or the other." She lied. Jayden's love for her resonated in everything he did.

Studying her facial expression, Dylan mumbled, "Did you make him fall in love with you?"

Chrissie moseyed to the sofa and sat down. She felt like a bug under a microscope. "No, he had a crush on me before my transformation. When I bit him, it intensified what he already felt."

"Will he always love you?"

Irritated with the direction of the questions, Chrissie's temper flashed. "I don't know for sure — maybe."

To her surprise, a wide grin spread across Dylan's face. He sauntered to the couch. "If you bit me, could you make me love you forever?"

"No, not if you didn't love me already. To some extent, I can control what you do. I can't control what you feel."

Dylan's eyes twinkled like stars on a clear summer's night when he sat next to her. "That's good to know."

The unexpected mood change contained a contagion. Chrissie grinned too. "Why?"

Pulling her hand to his heart, Dylan confessed. "Because when we fall in love, I want to be sure that it's real, and not just your magic."

Overjoyed, Chrissie beamed. "First, there is no magic involved, and second," her voice softened, "are you planning to fall in love?"

Dylan placed his palm on her cheek. "Yes indeed. I plan to sweep you off your feet." He sounded so natural, so matter-of-fact.

Chrissie found herself speechless. Dylan had already accomplished that task. Not knowing how to react, she focused on the grains in the glossy hardwood floor. During the lull in conversation, she heard the purr of her father's engine as he turned onto their private drive. "I hear my dad coming."

If her father's arrival upset Dylan, neither his heart rate nor his breathing gave any indication. "I know. I can hear his ride."

Stunned that he could hear the car from that distance, Chrissie's jaw dropped. "I didn't realize your hearing was as acute as mine."

Smug as ever, Dylan bragged, "I told you, I'm a warrior. We're trained to be observant." He kissed the end of her nose. "I'm one of the best." His self-confidence never wavered.

Chrissie listened with bated breath as William parked his BMW. She wondered what would happen when her dad came face to face with the guy she adored. Dylan stroked her hair and gazed at her reassuringly. Chrissie heard her dad hesitate before he slammed the door. As he marched into the kitchen, he mumbled under his breath.

"Dad," Chrissie called, as he entered the dining room, "We're in the family room." She could tell by her dad's gait that he also dreaded this moment. When she glanced up, Dylan sported a broad smile.

Briefcase in hand, William trudged into the family room with a scowl on his face. "Good evening. I see we have a guest."

Chrissie squirmed in her seat. "Yes. Dylan and I were just watching a little television."

Scrutinizing Dylan's every movement, William tossed his case in the recliner. "I can see that." He made no attempt at civility. "I understood you to say you were going to see a movie tonight."

"There wasn't anything playing, so we...."

Before Chrissie could finish her comment, Dylan broke in, "Professor Garrett, I owe you an apology. The last time I was here, my actions were reprehensible. I overreacted and I apologize."

Without sharing her private thoughts, Chrissie gazed at Dylan with total adoration. *"How could Father help but be impressed by his charms?"*

William folded his arms. "Well, young man, your actions were inexcusable." Chrissie wasn't expecting her father's statement at all. She wished she could hide until the confrontation was over. "But, I am willing to put our animosity aside for Chrissie's sake."

"Awesome." Dylan stood and extended his hand. "Can we call a truce?"

William shook Dylan's hand. "That will be acceptable." At first, he sounded like the C.E.O. of a major corporation. Then, he scowled. "As long as you treat my daughter well, we will have no problems." He tightened his grip on Dylan's hand. "If you hurt her, you *will* answer to me. Understood?" Chrissie had to admit she felt a little pleased that her dad reacted like an ordinary father.

"Yes sir." Dylan pulled his hand back. "You've made yourself quite clear."

"Good, see to it that you remember what I've said. Otherwise, you will have a serious problem." William scrutinized Dylan from head to foot one last time, then exited the room.

Chrissie sprang to her feet and laced her arm around Dylan's. "That wasn't so hard, was it?" Her confidence in his charm didn't disappoint.

"I guess not." He kissed her forehead. "We have a long way to go before he accepts our relationship."

Chrissie held his hand as she led the way to the couch. "Are we in a relationship?"

Dylan scooted next to her. With incredible alacrity, he placed his lips against her ear. The warmth of his breath sent shivers down her neck. She shuddered. He caressed her slender face in his huge hands. "Do you think you could get involved with someone like me?" His warm brown eyes seem to penetrate her soul.

Before Chrissie answered, she hesitated. "I'm already involved with you — since the moment we met." As he traced the contours of her lips, every nerve in her body trembled. The sensation traveled down her spine.

Tenderly, Dylan pressed his mouth against hers. "Can we consider this an exclusive relationship?"

She swallowed hard. "Yes."

He hooked his arms around her waist and embraced her. His lips burned against hers, and her body exploded with a passion she had never known. As the intensity of the kiss heightened, Chrissie felt Dylan's body tremble. She could hear his heart thundering inside his chest.

Gathering her strength, Chrissie pulled away from him. "You should go now." She panted, fighting to maintain self-control. "It's getting late."

Dylan raised her chin and sighed. "Do you really want me to go?"

"Yes." Knowing her father could hear everything made her extremely uncomfortable.

"Did I do something wrong?"

"No. You haven't done anything wrong. I need to talk to my father. This is all so new to him." She lowered her gaze. "*And me as well.*"

Dylan drew back and peered into her face. "You're right. I should go. I'm sure we're making your father very uncomfortable. Do you want me to talk to him with you?"

Chrissie marveled at his sensitivity. "Thanks. That's chivalrous of you, but this is one talk I need to have with him alone."

"Are you sure? I could act as your shield. My body's trained for battle."

Annoyed by the crudeness of his unexpected joke, Chrissie rolled her eyes. "I'm a big girl. I can express myself quite well without your assistance."

A frown crept across his face. "We've got to do something about that temper of yours." He kissed her forehead and then laughed. "Are you sure you don't want me to stay. I don't want you to face this alone."

"I'm fine. Dad will understand." She made the statement more to impress her father than Dylan.

Dylan stood and stretched. He reached for Chrissie's hand to help her to her feet. The couple held hands as they strolled to his truck. Before he opened the door, he kissed her softly. "I'll see you tomorrow."

Chrissie watched until Dylan had traveled the half-mile length of the driveway, then turned onto the highway. When she turned, her dad stood directly behind her. Clutching her chest, she jumped back. "I didn't hear you come up." The acuity of her senses had always been her pride. Now, it seemed she couldn't hear even the loudest sounds.

"I told you to hone your skills." He paused. "Speaking of hearing, did he just ask you to date him, exclusively?"

A twinge of annoyance raced through her. She braced herself for the unavoidable argument. "You know very well what he asked of me. After all, you were eavesdropping." Dylan had expressed his desire well. Now, she needed to handle her temper.

William's anger flared as well. "One cannot eavesdrop in his own house."

Nana had made that very statement when she started dating Jayden Ballenger. She had left out that bit of information when Dylan asked about her familiar. Realizing another argument would exasperate matters, she clasped her hands and brought them to rest on her lips. For a number of seconds, she paused. Her anger was getting out of control. "Let's both calm down. We can go inside to talk."

Chrissie led the way to the family room. This would be the ideal venue for their discussion. Folding her arms, she waited until her dad settled into the recliner, then she sat in the loveseat adjacent him. "Dad, I don't want to argue with you about this." She clasped her praying hands together. Although she hated to disappoint her father, the heart does what it wants to do. "You may as well know, I've decided to date Dylan. It doesn't matter what you say. I'm going to do it."

"Chrissie, you're too inexperienced to entertain the notion of dating one guy, especially someone you've only known a month."

"What?" Her face twisted into a clouded mass of anger. "Dad, I'm twenty-five years old. How old would you like me to be? I'm not your little girl, anymore. I'm a *grown woman*."

William waved his hand in front of his face as though he could erase his previous statement. "Okay, granted, you are old enough." He wavered for a second before he spoke. "What kind of relationship can you have? You're a vampire, and he's a—a. What—a dragon? Half dragon?" His head oscillated from side to side. "Think about what you're getting yourself into." Flaring nostrils testified to his indignation.

Chrissie leaned forward. "I've thought about this. It's what I want." She moistened her lips. "I don't know what will happen, but I've got to do this for myself."

"Peanut. I just want to protect you. You said yourself, he kills vampires. It's part of what he does."

"Daddy. I have feelings for Dylan. Feelings I need to explore." She shook her head. "You can't protect me from *my* emotions. No matter how much you want to. There are some things I have to experience for myself."

William stared into the fireplace. "This is not wise." The veins on his temples protruded so tightly they appeared ready to rupture. "I don't like it."

Concern gripped Chrissie. If her dad had been human, he might have had a heart attack. However, she did not relent. When she spoke, the cadence in her voice took a more reasonable tone. "I'm sorry you're so concerned." Determined to stand her ground, she bit her bottom lip. "I'm not asking you to like it. I'm asking you to let me live my life."

William joined Chrissie on the couch. He took her hand in his. "I can't stop you," he sighed, "so I'll trust your judgment."

Resting her head on her father's shoulder, Chrissie smiled weakly. "I love you, Daddy." The skirmish had ended for the moment, but she realized another battle loomed on the horizon.

~End of Volume One~

Transcending Dawn

Vampire Series

Volume Two

Shadows of Jealousy

By

Payton A. Whitfield

CONTENTS

VOLUME TWO ~ SHADOWS OF JEALOUSY

CHAPTER ONE

Acceptance

Dylan and Chrissie sat on the overstuffed, black loveseat in the family room, planning their weekend. Engrossed in the evening paper, William, her dad, lounged in the matching recliner, his feet planted atop the ottoman.

When he finished reading the newspaper, he folded it. The pages rustled as he creased the corners. Dylan glanced up from the television. His nightly visits had become routine. Even William seemed to enjoy his companionship. "May I borrow your paper?"

The relaxed atmosphere had changed from the initial hostility that existed between the two men. Chrissie stared at the pair in wonder. *"Never in my wildest dreams would I have imagined that the two men I love the most, would get along so well. Three months ago, I thought they'd kill each other in this very room."* She smiled in contentment.

Leaning forward, William extended the periodical. "Sure. I'm finished with it anyway."

Dylan grasped the paper. "Thanks, Doc."

William stretched with arms outspread. He rose from the leather chair and glanced at the lovebirds. "What are you kids doing this weekend?"

Flipping through the paper, Dylan answered, "We haven't decided yet." Atop the coffee table, he'd laid the editorial page and the entertainment sections of the issue.

When Dylan caught a glimpse of Chrissie's upturned lips, he asked, "What are you grinning about?"

She shook her head. "I was just thinking."

"About?"

Chrissie moved closer to Dylan, so near his thigh touched hers. "About how much things have changed. You two get along so well—even after Professor Marshall's campaign to poison Dad against you." Reclining against the sofa, she felt his hand envelop hers. "I swear; I can't understand why that man hates you so much." She massaged her temples. *"From that first day in his class, I could tell he despised Dylan, even before I realized he was a vampire. His ability to disguise his natural body odor threw me. I know what one vampire does affects every other, but that doesn't explain his extreme animosity toward Dylan."*

William strolled to the hearth. "I don't think Walter meant any real harm. True, his actions proved misguided. Nonetheless, I don't question his good intentions." He darted his eyes from Chrissie to Dylan. "Evidently, he heard about Dylan's reputation with the ladies. Since we're colleagues, he wanted to look out for my daughter. After all, vampires don't generally get involved with drachmons."

Like vampires, drachmons are creatures of legend. Descended from dragons, they possess great physical strength. Plus, their skill in battle far exceeds any other being.

As Chrissie watched her father, she drew her legs beneath her. "Personally, I don't understand his concern. I can date whomever I like. If you ask me, he's an old ear-hustler who likes to cause trouble. Thanks to his meddling, you and Dylan almost came to blows."

A scowl marred Dylan's handsome features, as he patted Chrissie's knee. "It does seem odd that he's so interested in you."

William lifted a Ming vase off the mantle, and then drew a white handkerchief from his trousers. Gingerly, he wiped the container's side. "Well, I'm headed to my study. I have to correct a few assignments; tomorrow will come quickly." He placed the urn in the exact space it had occupied.

William hesitated, and then sauntered toward the door.

"Good night, Dad." Chrissie leaned forward and reached for the entertainment section.

Immediately, William stopped walking. Though his back was turned, Chrissie could tell he was smiling. "Night, Peanut. Good night, Dylan."

Dylan lowered the paper. "Good night, Doc."

While Chrissie scanned the entertainment section, Dylan scrutinized the headlines. She glanced up. "Anything out of place tonight?"

Slightly lowering the paper, he answered, "Nope. Everything seems normal. Besides. If there's any supernatural activity, the council will contact me."

"Are you still determined to go if there's trouble?"

With a sigh, Dylan cut his eyes at her. "Chrissie. I don't have a choice. I've told you..."

"I know. I know." Using her fingers to form quotation marks, she mimicked his voice perfectly. "Anytime there's a threat of wholesale carnage to the human world it's your responsibility to defend them."

"That, my darling, is right, so stop suggesting that I shirk my duty." With a flick of her wrist, Chrissie shook the newspaper before her, gave Dylan a disapproving look, and then returned to her reading.

Dylan examined page after page, searching for any possible threat to humanity. Once he had perused the entire publication, he pitched it on the coffee table. With a twinkle in his eyes, he grinned. "Have you found anything you want to do yet?"

"Not yet." She tossed the periodical aside.

He wrapped his arm around Chrissie's shoulder. "I have an idea."

"What?" She gazed into his deep brown eyes. It didn't matter what they did. Time spent with Dylan provided her greatest joy.

"This weekend will mark our three month anniversary. Let's drive to Bossier. We can go to the Boardwalk. We'll find lots to do there."

Chrissie nestled her head against his chest. "Sound like a plan."

Suddenly, Dylan snapped his finger and pointed at her. "By the way, what do you want for our anniversary?"

She raised her head and gazed into his eyes. "You."

"You have me," he declared, "but I want to get you something special — something to commemorate how we feel about each other."

"Dylan," she softened her voice. "Just being with you is special enough. I don't need anything else."

"When we get to the Boardwalk, we'll hit some of the shops. You can pick out what you want then."

Since Dylan ignored the fact that she didn't want anything material, Chrissie shrugged. "This is Thursday, so I have time to think about what I want. Think about what you want as well."

He kissed her forehead. "One kiss from you means more to me than anything you could buy."

With her finger, Chrissie traced the outline of his collar. "If you're buying a gift for me, I'm buying one for you."

He placed his hand on her cheek. "I love you, Chrissie."

"I know," she murmured, content to linger in his arms forever, "and I love you." Sharing her feelings had never been easy. The death of her mother when she was ten, coupled with a lack of paternal involvement had left deep emotional scars. William had stayed out of her life for eighteen years. He didn't want her absorbed in the vampire world. However, when he learned she had terminal brain cancer, he initiated Chrissie into his sphere of existence.

CHAPTER TWO
Heartache

When Chrissie and Estefina stepped through the ornate double doors of Jefferson Hall, Chrissie wrinkled her brow. "Hum. I wonder where Dylan is." Most nights, when she got out of class, his six-three frame was resting against her car.

Estefina shrugged, her voice raspy. "Maybe his class ran late." Normally, her pink blouse made her brown eyes beam, but that night, the glow had dimmed into a dull lackluster hue. The winter trousers she wore were far too warm for such a balmy evening.

Chrissie nodded. "You're probably right." A light April breeze tousled her strawberry tresses. Out of habit, she zipped her hoodie. The smell of pine filled her lungs, and she stretched her arms in satisfaction. "Why don't we hang out at the Shack until he gets out?" Estefina glared straight ahead, and remained quiet. "Estefina. Did you hear me?"

Estefina blinked twice. "Huh? What?"

Chrissie slung her backpack over her shoulder. "I said, let's go to the Shack until Dylan gets out of class."

"Sure."

Estefina never passed up an opportunity to comment on anything. Chrissie's concern escalated. "Why don't we walk?"

Without meeting Chrissie's gaze, she answered, "Okay."

"What's wrong? You've been out of it all evening."

"Nothing's wrong. I'm fine."

"You're not telling me the truth. Your eyes are red, and you sound distracted."

Estefina shrugged. "I'm fine. Don't worry about me."

The young women strolled the two blocks in silence. Only the rustle of Chrissie's jeans and the click of her heels against the pavement disturbed the quiet. Estefina stared at the ground the entire course. As they stepped onto the lot, Chrissie surveyed the cars. "Wow. Looks like everyone in the dorm skipped the cafeteria's food tonight."

Rhythmic thumps emanated from the busy establishment. The pair ambled across the parking lot. When they arrived, Estefina opened the door and peeked inside. "The place is packed. I don't know if we can get in there."

Thrilled by the crowd, Chrissie smiled to herself. At the beginning of the spring term, William had purchased the Shack for her. She thought it more prudent not to tell anyone. Even

Dylan didn't know Chrissie owned the club.

Chrissie stood on tiptoes, her eyes in search of an empty seat. "There's one," she said, pointing to the back of the room. They pushed through the dense mob. Before she sat down, Chrissie scanned the dance floor. There, she spotted Matt Jenkins with Jennifer Fletcher. *"Darn. I hope Estefina doesn't see them. She's been depressed enough lately. The last thing she needs is to see Matt with Jenny."* They scooted into their booth. Chrissie studied Estefina's face. She could tell her wounds ran deep. *"I wonder what happened. I don't usually get involved in other people's dilemmas, but Estefina is my best friend. Maybe a frank discussion will help."*

With her eyes shut, Estefina swayed to and fro with the music. Though tempted, Chrissie decided not to bother her. However, once the melody ended, she ignored her better judgment and leaned forward. "Estefina, do you mind if I ask you a question?" She laced her fingers. "You don't have to answer if it makes you uncomfortable."

Estefina jerked her head upwards. A scowl marred her classic Hispanic beauty. "What do you want to know?"

In a pitch so soft no one else could hear, Chrissie probed. "I don't mean to pry." She moistened her lips. "But, what's going on between you and Matt?"

Estefina didn't answer.

"You've been too quiet lately. That isn't like you. Maybe it would help if you talked about what's bothering you."

At that instant, the waitress appeared. She slapped the menus on the table. When she turned to flit away, she muttered over her shoulder. "I'll be back in a couple of minutes to take your order."

Estefina picked up the menu. She pushed at the corners with her fingernail. The plastic coating peeled back. Like an angry child, she tossed the cardboard on the table. "I found out Matt has been dating Jenny behind my back."

Slack jawed, Chrissie gasped. "I didn't realize the breakup was that serious." The couple had dated all through high school. To avoid four years of separation, they chose the same college. Everyone thought they made the perfect couple. Stunned, she sat back in her seat. "Are you sure?" Chrissie shook her head. *"That was a stupid question."*

"Yes. I confronted him, and he confessed. He says he still loves me." Tears ran down Estefina's cheeks. "According to him, he got involved with her because I wouldn't have sex with him." She wiped her eyes, and black mascara streaked her fingers.

Chrissie ogled Matt, who seemed to be having a blast. "Would you like to go someplace else?"

With her elbow on the table, Estefina rested her chin on her palm. "No. Matt is not going to ruin my life. I won't give him that pleasure."

For several minutes, the two sat in silence. Chrissie contemplated the best way to help her friend. "Do you think you can ever forgive him?"

Estefina slumped her shoulders, and lowered her gaze. Masses of silky brunette hair swept across her face. "I don't know." Tears glistened in her dark eyes. "I want to." She narrowed her eyes. "How can I trust him after this?"

"Has he asked you to forgive him?"

"Yes, but I don't trust him anymore." She glanced around the room as though someone was listening. "Could you forgive Dylan if he did this to you?"

Chrissie frowned. "To tell the truth, I don't know. I might. If he apologized, and I thought he was sincere." She pulled a napkin from the holder, then absently tore it to shreds. "I'm not sure, maybe."

Estefina stuck her index finger in her mouth. Grazing the loose skin of the knuckle, she snatched it out. "I'm so confused right now. I don't know what I want, or what I think." She glanced at Matt, who had his lips pressed against Jenny's ear.

"Take your time. Think about it." Chrissie scratched the back of her head, then smoothed the ruffled hair. "I believe he loves you. I'd hate to see your relationship end over a fling."

From the dance floor, Matt glared at Estefina. With a flick of her head, she turned to face Chrissie. "I'm not sure it's worth saving."

Chrissie tilted her head to the side. From the distance, she heard Matt talking to Jenny. "Will you excuse me for a minute?" he asked.

Matt stumbled to their booth and stood over Estefina. The scent of alcohol permeated the air. "Can I talk to you for a minute?"

Chrissie had never seen Matt drink anything stronger than a Coke. She found his uncharacteristic behavior rather disconcerting.

Estefina placed the back of her hand against her nose. "What do you want, Matt? You've got a date. Go back and talk to her."

Through bloodshot eyes, Matt scowled at Estefina. "Look. We have things to talk about." Saliva spewed from his mouth. "I need to see you in private."

"Sober up, and maybe I'll talk to you. You're in no shape to talk to me or anybody else right now." Attempting to pull her from the booth, Matt grabbed Estefina's arm. She braced herself against the back of the seat. "No, Matt!"

Under her breath, Chrissie growled. Her best friend's heart was racing, and she smelled of fear. Unable to restrain herself any longer, she sprang to her feet and stood eye level with Matt. For a split second, she considered knocking him on his rear.

Instead, she decided to reason with him. "Matt. Now is probably not the best time to talk with Estefina. You should wait until you're in a better frame of mind."

Matt swayed, and stumbled backwards. "Well, well. Chrissie Garrett. Who are you — to tell me — what to do?"

Chrissie feigned a smile. "I'm your friend, Matt."

"Well, *friend*, let me give *you* some advice." When Matt enunciated his words, moisture sprinkled Chrissie's forehead. The foul odor of stale alcohol offended her nostrils, and she turned her head. "People who live in glass houses shouldn't throw sticks.

Her arms folded, Chrissie giggled. "That's a mixed metaphor, silly. It's stones."

"W,whatever," Matt stammered. "The point is. Don't get involved in *my* relationship until you straighten out your own."

Hearing Matt's words, Chrissie bristled. "What are you talking about?"

Estafina rose from her seat. "Shut up, Matt."

Matt wobbled his head toward Estefina. "No. She's in *my* business. She's got a right to know." He turned to face Chrissie. Immediately, she saw her reflection in his drunken, glossy eyes. "Your precious Dylan isn't so perfect." His face contorted as if he smelled something foul. "Wonder where he is tonight, huh?"

Livid, Estefina's breaths grew louder. "If you say another word, Matthew Jenkins," she grumbled through clenched teeth, "I'll never speak to you again."

The full import of what Matt was saying collided with Chrissie's thoughts. *"If what Matt implies is true, both the man I love, and my best friend, have betrayed me."* She leered at her companion. "Estefina. What is he talking about?"

"He's not talking about anything, Chrissie. I swear." Estefina rolled her eyes at Matt. "He's drunk. Don't pay him any attention."

Matt staggered. "I'm not so drunk, huh?" With his index finger pressed to his temple, he sneered. Well, maybe I can remember what Kaylee said." He snapped his fingers. "Oh yeah, I remember. She's planned a surprise for Dylan tonight. She's his personal gift." With a twist of the knife, he smirked. "I'm not saying he invited her over, *but* if he's so special, where is he?" Estefina turned red with rage. "What's the matter, Christina?" The venom rolled from Matt's tongue, crushing Chrissie in its wake. "You look a little green around the gills."

Furious and devastated, Chrissie shuddered. "Estefina. Is Matt telling the truth?"

Before Estefina confirmed his story, she stared daggers at Matt. "Kaylee did boast that she would get Dylan back. She said she'd give herself to him, if that's what it took to get him."

Matt's words had waved a red flag in front of a charging bull. Unsure of where to direct her rage, Chrissie lashed out at her friend. "You knew this all the time, and said nothing? I thought we were closer than that."

"I'm your friend." Estefina's pleaded with Chrissie to understand. "How could I tell you something like that? Besides, Dylan is too smart to play Kaylee's games. You know that."

Tears welled in Chrissie's eyes, but they didn't fall. "So, that's why you asked if I could forgive Dylan?" Like an Olympic sprinter, she bolted for the exit. Fear of what she might do if she stayed frightened her. Hurling Matt through the wall would have been easy; it required self-restraint to leave.

Propelled by rage and jealousy, Chrissie ran toward the door. To maintain a human gait, she exerted extraordinary effort. As she burst through the exit, she overheard Estefina say, "Matthew Jenkins, don't you ever speak to me again. How could you deliberately hurt a friend, especially one who is trying to help us? This is unforgiveable. I never want to see you again."

* * * *

Chrissie parked two blocks from Dylan's apartment. If she pulled onto his street, he would recognize the sound of her engine.

Under the cloak of darkness, Chrissie zipped down the shadowy street. In less than thirty seconds, she'd covered the expanse. When she reached his building, she crept to the rear. Like a common criminal, she skulked in the darkness, and then hid behind a huge oak tree. Though ashamed of her actions, she needed to know what was actually happening.

From the distance, she heard Kaylee plead. "Don't you want to be with me at all?" Fury stung Chrissie's face. Through the window, she could see that Kaylee stood about a foot from Dylan. The tight burgundy sweater she wore clung to her, its v-neck exposing her robustness. A short black skirt and matching stockings made her legs appear even longer than they were. Chrissie smashed her fist against the side of the tree. Shattered by the force, huge chunks splintered away. *"From here, her head would make an easy target. I should pull a brick from the building, and shatter her empty skull."*

Head upturned, Chrissie focused on the pair. From her vantage point, she could see everything.

"Kaylee." Dylan's relaxed-fit jeans rustled as he backed away. "I don't want to use you." He faced the window. "That's all it would be." Smirking, Chrissie placed her hand over her frozen heart.

"And what if I want you to use me?"

Dylan frowned. "There's nothing between us.

There never really was."

Kaylee eased forward, diminishing the distance between them. "I don't believe that, Dylan. No matter what you say, I know you cared for me."

She tried to place her hand on Dylan's shoulder. He blocked her with his arm, then stepped back. "The operative word here is *cared*, past tense."

"So you're saying you never loved me." Chrissie smiled with satisfaction. She felt sorry for Kaylee—well, almost.

"Look." He stepped around Kaylee and walked to the couch. "I'm sorry if I misled you. I never meant for that to happen."

Several seconds passed before Kaylee spoke. "I love you, Dylan."

Chrissie crouched, and snarled aloud. *"When she comes out, I'm going to rip her throat out."* She shook her head. *"Nah. Her blood would probably sour on my stomach."*

As he sat on the sofa, Dylan scowled. "You don't love me. You don't even know me."

Although Kaylee flinched, she persisted. "I know all I need to know."

"No. You don't." His tone softened. "Not like Christina."

Hearing Dylan's tender confession, Chrissie's heart softened. Her rage subsided; she swelled with pride.

Kaylee sat next to him. "Why are you so attracted to her?"

Dylan stared at Kaylee. "Chrissie knows me. She knows everything about me, and she loves me anyway." The leather sofa creaked as he stood. "She's seen the worst in me, and she still loves me. I've seen the worst in her, and I still love her." In the corner, Dylan had a set of weights. He strolled over to retrieve one. "That's what love is—knowing the worst about a person, and loving them in spite of it."

Kaylee turned up her nose. "I've heard about that temper of hers."

A hardy laugh erupted deep within Dylan. "Yes. She does have quite a temper." He flexed his muscle, straining the fabric in his blue t-shirt, then set the weight down. "Don't you see; I love that about her. She's the strongest woman I've ever known. Well, other than my mother. If she found out you were here, she'd probably tear my head off." He strolled over to the window, and Chrissie crouched behind the gigantic oak. Abruptly, he pulled the curtain back.

Kaylee bounced to her feet. "That's what you love about her—her bad temper? Please tell me you're kidding."

Dylan turned to face her. "You missed the point, Kaylee. She has the strength of her conviction." He rested his palms on the window frame. "If she thinks something is wrong, she's not afraid to voice her opinion. I've seen her stand up to her dad, even when she knew she couldn't win." With deliberate steps, he sauntered back to the couch and straddled the arm.

Kaylee elevated her chest. "Are you saying, you think I'm weak?"

"I don't know what you are. I've never taken the time to find out."

Her face turned bright red. When Chrissie spotted her shocked expression, she glowed inside. Without another word, Kaylee slapped his face. She stormed out of the room, slamming the door behind her.

Dylan walked to the window, and then opened it. Gazing into Chrissie's face, he called, "You can come up now, sweetheart."

Busted.

Even though Chrissie felt silly for having her attempt at espionage discovered, she experienced a great sense of joy. She leaped through the window and landed inches from him. "How did you know I was out there?"

"I heard you as soon as you came up. Your father's right. You need to hone your skills." She punched his arm. As if experiencing great pain, he grimaced playfully and then rubbed his shoulder. He took Chrissie into his arms. "Besides, I knew when I didn't meet you at your car, you'd find a reason to look for me."

"I don't think I like your taking me for granted." She pretended to pout. *"Truthfully, I'm thrilled. He knows me so well."*

Dylan kissed her. His aroma was sweet, yet masculine. No chemist could capture his natural fragrance. "I'm not taking you for granted, my darling. I just know you well. Very well." He winked her.

Chrissie had to catch her breath. Now, she understood Kaylee's reluctance to let him go. Though nothing would have pleased her more than cuddling in his arms, she pushed his chest to loosen his grip. "What was Kaylee doing here?"

To close the gap she created, Dylan tightened his arms around her. His heart pounded at her proximity, and she rejoiced. "Weren't you listening?" he whispered, kissing her neck.

Despite the desire surging through her body, Chrissie persisted. "I heard some of the conversation," she murmured, as she ran her hand over his broad chest, "but I still don't know why she was here."

Dylan ran his lips along her neck and nibbled her ear. Under his touch, Chrissie's defenses crumbled. In his most seductive tone, he admitted the obvious. "She showed up at my door, hoping to rekindle a romance."

"That did it." In an instant, his passionate touch was transformed into rage. Using her full strength, Chrissie shoved him away. "Really? So there *was* something between you, and that tramp."

The calm expression on Dylan's face did not falter. "Not really. Besides, I told you about her the day we met."

His serene demeanor made Chrissie angrier. "Did you sleep with her, Dylan?" Although she wanted the truth, she feared the answer.

The accusation seemed to annoy him. He sighed and rolled his eyes. "Christina, I love you. But, the past is over." Marching to his small leather loveseat, Dylan plopped down. "What happened in the past should stay there. I don't want to know who you slept with, and I'd never ask. What good would it serve, other than to upset me?" He patted the cushion next to him.

Frustration and stubbornness prevented Chrissie from enjoying that pleasure—and, yes it would have been much to her liking. "I've never slept with anyone. Can you say that?"

Springing from the couch, Dylan stormed toward the kitchen. "I'm not having this conversation."

"Well, I'll go home."

Contrary to her expectations, Chrissie's hollow threat did not seem to impress him. He turned on his heels. "Maybe you should."

Chrissie darted for the window. Before she could make the leap, Dylan wrapped his massive arms around her, and pulled her back inside.

When she turned to face him, she shoved his chest. "What are you doing?"

He gazed into her hazel eyes, his tone loving. "I don't want you to go. Stay and I'll answer any questions you have. I have nothing to hide from you."

The muscles in Chrissie's back relaxed. She allowed Dylan to pull her near. "Are you sure? You seemed so adamant a minute ago."

"Don't you understand what you mean to me? If it's that important for you to know, I'll tell you."

Chrissie required only a second of contemplation. "*As he said, the past is dead. It should remain buried. You can't move forward if you're constantly gawking at what lies behind you.*" The fight ended as quickly as it started. His willingness to share had quenched her craving for details. She focused on his biceps. "That's alright. I've decided I don't want to know."

A sigh of relief escaped his lips. "Thank you." He reached for Chrissie's hand. "You are the most important thing in my life. I can't rewrite the past. I wish I could, but I can't."

He placed her hand over his heart. "Since the moment I set eyes on you, there's been no one else for me. From this point on, I promise I will love you faithfully, for as long as we exist."

All of Chrissie's lingering doubts evaporated. Nothing. Absolutely nothing, would ever separate them. No test, no trial, no temptation—nothing would ever sever the iron grip that secured her heart.

CHAPTER THREE
Troubled Relationships

As the couple whizzed down the snakelike back roads leading to the beach, the exquisite beauty of the countryside awed Chrissie. Though the darkness cast no shadows on the landscape, she could see the pine trees swaying in the gentle breeze. Purple horse mints with lavender blooms danced along the highway. Likewise, the crisp aroma of mint and lemon filled the evening air.

Chrissie lay back in the seat, and gazed at Dylan. "I'm glad we decided to drive to the lake." She closed her eyes and inhaled, an air of serenity wafted across her lips.

"Me too. There's nothing like the open air to sooth your nerves after a fight."

She focused on the royal blue cap that concealed his curly mane. "I'm sorry about the fight. It was stupid."

"I'm sorry too. Once we're on neutral ground, we can have a discussion about a certain person's jealousy." Trees zoomed past as he downshifted around a hairpin curve, and then turned unto the entrance.

"Jealousy? Me? I don't know what you're talking about," she mused.

When Dylan parked the car, Chrissie turned on her iPod to craft the perfect atmosphere. The tension between them had been palpable. They both needed to relax. Dylan reclined his seat and tilted his head back. Chrissie turned her head toward the window to digest the many sounds of the night. The wind whistled through the evergreen, and waves crashed along the shore. Crickets chirped in the underbrush, celebrating the unusually warm spring weather. Smiling in contentment, she removed her gray hoodie.

Once the tension had floated away, Chrissie gathered her courage. "Why are you so quiet tonight?"

With his eyes still closed, Dylan answered, "Just thinking."

"What are you thinking about?"

He opened his eyes. The corners of his lips exploded into an upward turn. "About how lucky I am."

Chrissie glowed, confident that he was referring to her. "In what way are you lucky?"

He glanced at her, adoration sparkled in his eyes. "I have the sweetest woman in the world by my side, and she loves me."

"I don't know how sweet she is." Chrissie laid

her palm against his cheek. "But she definitely loves you."

He placed his hand atop hers. "You are sweet."

She chuckled. "Yeah, right."

His arm over the steering wheel, Dylan sat up straight so he could face her. "I tease you about your temper, but you're one of the most sensitive women I've ever met."

Angling her body toward his, she replied, "Being sensitive doesn't make me sweet. Dad says I'm one *mean* child."

"First of all, Christina, you are *not* a child. You're a vibrant and beautiful woman. Secondly, you have to be mean to deal with *your* dad." He clenched his teeth in a gruesome grin. Together, they laughed at his unorthodox humor. "Seriously, you are wonderful. You're a little head strong, but that's what I need. Who else could deal with me?"

"Dylan. I think the moonlight and the music are getting to you."

He lifted her chin. "Nope, I realize how lucky I am to have you."

"I'm the lucky one."

With a finger, he traced the contour of her lips, then leaned in and kissed her. Each time he caressed her, Chrissie's physical reaction intensified. She quivered at the sound of his racing heart. When he released her, he spoke softly. "Let's walk along the shore."

While Chrissie struggled to regain her composure, Dylan exited the car. He moved to the passenger side, and opened the door. His movements rivaled those of a gazelle. Ever the gentleman, he extended his hand to assist her. "Just a second," she said, and grabbed her bag. Reaching inside, she retrieved a hair band, piled her tresses atop her head, then secured it into a ponytail. To check her appearance, she pulled down the sun visor, which housed a mirror. She chuckled.

"What are you sniggling about?"

Examining her style, Chrissie turned her head from one side to the other. "I was just thinking about how foolish some human myths are."

"What particular myth did you have in mind?" Dylan raised his cap, then secured it snugly.

She snatched one last peek. "Oh. I think it's funny that people believe vampires can't see themselves in the mirror. How can something solid cast no reflection?" Satisfied with her hair, she flipped the visor back in place. "I'm ready. But, I think I'll leave my purse in the trunk."

Dylan reached for her hand. "Alright. Sounds good." Once Chrissie exited the vehicle, Dylan closed the door with his free hand. After depositing her handbag in the trunk, they strolled down a well-traveled path.

Hand in hand, they wandered along the lake, their footsteps as silent as the grave. While they explored the 16,000 acre expanse, the couple savored the sights and sounds of nature. The hoot of a distant owl and the flutter of its wings filled the night as it swooped down to target its prey. A turtle inched its way along the shoreline, then burrowed a hole in the sand to hide itself from view. A white-tailed deer grazed in a field of lush green grass, while its fawn frolicked in the clearing. The pair melded with their environment. Though different species, Dylan and Chrissie were as much a part of nature as the birds in the air, or the fish in the stream.

Chrissie paused and gazed at Dylan. "I love you."

Without hesitation, he reciprocated. "I love you more."

Dylan wrapped his arms around Chrissie and drew her close. When he kissed her, there was even more passion than before. Warm pulsations coursed throughout her entire being. Not only did it encompass her body but the very essence of her soul. Again, Chrissie listened as his heart pounded. She smiled when the tempo of his breathing increased.

Aware she could easily lose control alone with Dylan in the dark, she pulled away. In search of a distraction, Chrissie darted her eyes from side to side. She pointed to the only object she could find. "Why don't we climb to the peak of that mountain?"

Dylan guffawed. "That isn't a mountain; it's a hill. Besides," he teased as he tapped the tip of her nose, "it might be better to go for a swim and cool off."

Chrissie pushed his shoulder. "Ha, ha."

"I have a better idea." He stretched his muscular leg behind him like an Olympic sprinter. "Let's race to the top."

A devilish impulse struck her. She pushed past him, and then sprinted away at top speed. Dylan bolted after her, hot on her heels before she covered a mile. Chrissie listened for his heartbeat. She reasoned the exertion would increase its rate and slow his gait. However, its rhythm remained steady. The stallion's pace increased.

Exhilarated by the wind whipping her face, Chrissie reached the top in record time. A delicate mixture of pine, honeysuckle, and mint filled her lungs. Never before had she noticed the wonderful aroma of nature's perfume. Everything seemed so new, so fresh, and so sweet. Perhaps, the change of seasons was responsible for the pungency of the fragrance. More likely, the change had taken place in her.

Just as the two reached the apex, Dylan leaped into the air. He grabbed her from behind, tucked her close to his body, and then tumbled to the ground. When he hit the earth, his cap flew from his head. Amazed by his dexterity, Chrissie fixed her eyes on his face. For a moment, she took in the hard contours of his face, basking in his masculinity. Dylan rose on his elbows, lifting her with him. "What's wrong?"

In her eyes, Dylan had always been handsome. In the soft shadows of the moonlight, Chrissie found herself enraptured by his exquisiteness. His strong chiseled jaw created the perfect frame for his full lips. Long lashes almost touched his thick brows. She pushed his disheveled hair out of his face. His rock-hard abs and the line of his long muscular body rivaled Adonis. "Nothing's wrong," she replied, finally answering his question. Blinking, she turned her head to the side. "Can't I look at you without there being something wrong?"

"Why were you looking at me like that?"

Unable to fabricate a good excuse, she placed her head against his upper body. "Are you fishing for a compliment?"

"No. It just makes me nervous when you stare at me like that."

To avoid his gaze, Chrissie focused on an ant mound. "If you must know, I was admiring your body."

The natural arch of his brows slanted upward. "What?"

Chrissie ran her fingers through the grass. "I was admiring your body. You have a perfect physique."

He sat up. "Thanks. But you are the perfect one. I love the red highlights in your ringlets, and your lips — absolutely luscious. I don't even compare with you." He swept Chrissie's hair behind her shoulders and then kissed her forehead. "You know, I didn't realize how long your hair was, until you flat ironed it."

This time Chrissie focused on his shirt. "If memory serves me correctly, you didn't care for my straight hair."

"You are gorgeous, no matter how you wear your hair." Dylan ran his fingers through her locks. "I happen to prefer it natural." He twirled one of her curls. "Those thick ringlets — I don't know — there's something about them, I love."

She laughed. "What is this, a mutual admiration society?"

"It sounds like it, doesn't it?"

As Chrissie cuddled against his neck, she noticed the gold chain Dylan always wore inside his shirt. She stroked it. "Dylan, what's this?"

Touching it, he answered, "This? It's a medallion."

"May I see it?"

"Sure." He pulled the pendant off, and held it up.

"It's lovely." She ran her finger over its surface.

"It's a family heirloom. It's been passed down for generations. Someday, I'll pass it on to my son."

Chrissie flipped the piece over, touched its raised etching, and marveled. "It's a dragon, flying over a village. Does it have some particular significance?"

"Yes. The dragon represents our clan of warriors, and the village represents the humans we protect."

"Wow."

"It reminds me of my obligations. No matter where I am, I'm aware I have a responsibility to fulfill."

Chrissie slid her fingers along the length of the chain. "What would happen if one day, you decided not to fulfill your duty?" She tugged at the hem of her lavender blouse. "Suppose you had something, or *someone* you didn't want to leave?"

"That would never happen." He took the medallion from her hand. "I have a sworn duty that I cannot neglect. If we have a future, you need to understand the depth of my commitment."

She placed her hand atop his. The medallion was suspended between his fingers. "But what if I didn't want you to go?"

"Chrissie." He frowned. "I don't have a choice.

It's my duty. No matter how much I love you, I would be forced to leave. This is my destiny.

In unison, they turned their heads at the sound of a doe. The delicate creature loped out of the brush and into the open field. Her reddish brown fur was barely visible in the moonlight. Yet, her white underbelly shone against the April moon. Dylan lifted Chrissie off his lap. He stood to his feet as quiet as a grasshopper in a field. Confused by his movements, Chrissie sighed. Protesting silently, Dylan placed one finger to his lips.

He inched toward the animal. "Be very still." The doe twitched her ears. "Don't frighten her." Reluctant even to breathe, Chrissie froze in place.

The deer eased closer to Dylan. At intervals, she paused to roll her big brown eyes in Chrissie's direction. With her white tail erect, the doe made her apprehension of Chrissie's presence clear.

As the creature approached, Dylan's eyes danced. She sniffed the air around him, and then advanced. Their interaction revealed some mystical bond between them. It was clear—the doe believed Dylan posed no threat. He stroked the white band just behind her nose. Hesitantly, she finally placed her face in his hands.

Sitting motionless in the grass, Chrissie watched in amazement as Dylan played with the deer. He spent the next hour frolicking with his new found friend.

Childish notions buzzed in Chrissie's brain. *"We came to spend time alone, not to play nursery games with some deer."* She shook her head to dislodge the jealousy. *"What immature thoughts."* Though she realized the foolishness of her reaction, she shouted, "Hey, don't I get any more attention?"

Startled by the tone of Chrissie's voice, her rival scampered away. After watching his playmate scurry into the underbrush, Dylan returned to Chrissie. Disappointment marred his striking countenance. "Why did you do that?" He picked up his cap, which had fallen off when he tackled her.

"I was lonely, Dylan." She pretended to pout. "I didn't come up here to share you with some deer."

As he shoved his cap atop his cascading curls, he mumbled, "You're so silly sometimes." He plopped down next to her

"I know." She shrugged. "So sue me. I got your attention, didn't I? "

With light-hearted humor, Dylan chuckled. "I've been neglecting you, huh?"

Chrissie smiled. "Yes, you have, and I don't like it. I'm supposed to be the center of your universe."

"Arrogant little missy, aren't you."

"Well, yeah," she teased, "I've been around you too long. Your conceit is rubbing off on me."

He winked. "Nothing wrong with self-confidence, babe."

"You should know." Chrissie snatched his hat from his head. In a flash, she darted away.

"You're in trouble now." He sprinted after her at full speed. Just as he leaped for her, she swerved to avoid him.

Slack-jawed, he marveled. "How did you do that?"

Chrissie grinned, astonished by his statement. The delight in her voice resounded. "Do what?"

Suddenly, Dylan's demeanor hardened. "No one can elude me. No one has ever been fast enough."

Knowing Dylan's customary style, Chrissie turned his cap backwards and placed it on his head. "There. Just like you like it." She smoothed her ruffled jeans. "I studied your moves the first time you tackled me. Then, I corrected accordingly. Don't forget; I'm a natural athlete myself."

He nodded. "Impressive."

Acknowledging the compliment, she curtsied. "Thank you, sir."

Dylan sat down on the grass and patted his lap. Without hesitation, Chrissie flew into his waiting arms. He held her close, and she nestled her head against his neck. In his arms, she was whole. No woman had ever been so satisfied.

While Dylan held her close, he kissed her hair. "Christina."

With eyes closed, she murmured, "Huh?"

"I need to know something."

Unaware of his thoughts, she kissed his neck. "Ok, what is it?"

He leaned back to inspect her face. "You told me your familiar is male."

"*Uh oh.*" Chrissie's imagination raced. "*I should have known — he called me Christina. This is not going to be good. I stepped in this one.*" She sighed. "Yes."

"Well, who is he? I mean, what's his name?"

The conversation headed down a slippery slope. Certain aspects of her relationship with Jayden would undoubtedly cause complications. In frustration, she threw up her hands. "Do we need to talk about him now?"

Dylan's tone remained calm. "Not if you don't want to." He pulled a blade of grass from the ground. "However, I would like to know."

Curling her fists, she grimaced. "Why?"

"It's a male thing. Humor me."

With a loud groan, Chrissie sighed. "His name is Jayden, Jayden Ballenger."

Dylan picked imaginary lint from her blouse.

"How old is he?"

"He's." Chrissie's scratched her head. "Uhh." She averted her eyes. Though unnecessary, she pretended she needed to calculate Jayden's age. "I think he's about twenty-eight." She knew precisely how old he was. Jayden had been her first love.

A sea of creases crested the center of Dylan brow. "Do you ever see him?"

Focusing on a field flower, she answered, "I haven't seen him since I moved here. I left him in Pinole to watch my grandmother."

"Where's that?"

"Is this inquisition ever going to end?" She moistened her lips. "It's in California."

Dylan stiffened. *"So,* is he still in love with you?"

"I thought we covered this once before. I told you I can't be sure. Maybe. Can we talk about something else?"

Dylan narrowed his eyes, and the muscles in his jaw flexed. "One last question."

"What is it?"

"If you sent for him today, would he come?"

"Yes, Dylan. Yes, he would. Now, can we talk about something else?"

He lifted her chin, forcing her eyes to meet his. "Why do you have such a hard time talking about this, if it's so innocent?"

Before she replied, Chrissie bit her bottom lip. "It makes me uncomfortable. Like you told me, there are some things we can't undo. That doesn't mean I want to dwell on them."

A slight growl rose from Dylan's chest. "Did you have feelings for him?"

Chrissie massaged her temples. "Growing up, I had a crush on him." She swallowed the lump in her throat. "But I got over it, years ago."

"Did you date him?"

She lowered her gaze. Her long locks hid her face. "Yes, but only once."

"But you did..."

She threw up her arms. "Stop already. Unless you want me to interrogate you about Kaylee, you need to halt the inquisition. Why are you so interested?" His line of questioning exasperated her beyond belief. The memory of her rival seared her brain. *"I guess this is how Dylan felt when I grilled him about Kaylee."*

He raised his head toward the dark sky. "I guess maybe I'm a little jealous."

"Jealous? Jealous of what?"

He pulled her near and explained. "There's a

man out there, who would quite probably die for you."

"And your point is?"

"Don't you understand how that makes me feel? I love you. I don't ever want to share you, with anyone."

"What? Dylan. You don't share me with anyone." She shook her head. "You never will. Jayden is my familiar. That's not the kind of relationship we have. He's like uh," she hesitated, as she struggled to articulate her thoughts, "a very close friend, who helps me when I need him."

Dylan placed his forehead against hers. "In a way, it's still a relationship. He's in love with you."

"I can't help that," she whined. "Besides, he's in California. Why borrow trouble?"

"You're right." Dylan smiled. "I'm sorry. I'm making such an issue of this. I promise to do better." The emotional thunderstorm subsided, as rapidly as it had blown in.

"I guess I've been a little jealous, too."

Dylan gave her a grave expression. "Speaking of jealousy, how did you know Kaylee was at my apartment tonight?"

"Oh." Seated on his lap, Chrissie sat up straight. "Matt and Estefina were having an argument. Like an idiot, I intervened. Matt took offense to my interference. I guess he wanted to hurt me, so he told me about Kaylee's plans."

Bursts of emerald sparked in Dylan's eyes. "He did what?"

"He told me I should take care of my own relationship, before I interfered with his."

"Why, that dirty — no good, little drone." Dylan clenched his fists so tightly the veins protruded. "How dare he start trouble between us! And your immediate response was to catch me in the act."

"No." Chrissie pleaded. "I wasn't trying to catch you in the act."

His drew his lips, exposing sharp, extended canines. "Then why did you show up at my apartment?"

"I needed the truth, Dylan. I've never been in love before — not like this. I needed to know that my confidence wasn't misplaced."

"So, you're saying you don't trust me."

Frustrated and angry, she closed her eyes. When she opened them, she explained, "I'm not saying that at all. I've seen how Kaylee pursues you. She's relentless, and I know you've been with her."

Brow knit together, Dylan raised his volume. "I never told you that."

Anger reared its ugly head. "You didn't have to." Chrissie's breathing increased. "It was obvious.

You told me you would change some things in your past."

"Wait just one minute." Dylan's breath came in rapid bursts. "There are things in your past that you would change too. Jayden for instance."

As though he had slapped her, Chrissie's face burned with rage. "How dare you compare my relationship with Jay, to you and that..." She could think of no appropriate description that would not have been derogatory. "...that female. I have never slept with Jay, or with anyone else for that matter. Can you say that?"

Dylan clenched his jaws. A rumble emanated from deep inside his chest. "I'm not going down that road with you."

"*Fine.* I'm going down a road—one that leads back to my house." Chrissie jumped to her feet. "Take me home." As she stormed away, Dylan grabbed her wrist. Infuriated by his physical contact, she turned on him. "Let me go."

Dylan gritted his teeth. His pointed incisors grazed his lower lip. "Not until we get this straight." He took a deep breath, and then let it out. "Christina, we're both angry. We're saying things we don't mean. Let's sit down and talk about this rationally."

Chrissie tried to snatch her arm from his grasp. It didn't budge. His strength far exceeded hers. "I don't want to talk to you rationally, or any other way. Let me go."

He tightened his grip. "I'll let you go if you promise to hear me out."

Although Chrissie was still angry, she realized Dylan was right. *"If our relationship has any hopes of succeeding, we need to be truthful."* She closed her eyes. "Alright."

He released her wrist, and then motioned for her to sit down. She plopped down on the cool grass, and Dylan joined her. "Chrissie, I would never do anything to hurt you. I hope you know that. I didn't know Kaylee was planning to show up at my apartment, but in a way, I'm glad she did."

In one move, Chrissie leaped to her feet. "What?"

Dylan grabbed her wrist again. "Just listen. I needed to get this straight, once and for all. Maybe, now she'll understand how much I love you. I've never been in love before." He released Chrissie's wrist. "Until now."

"You've never been in love before?" Hearing his admission, Chrissie was engulfed with joy. She sat down beside him.

"No, I've never been in love." He placed his powerful hand on her cheek. "Others have filled my time, but they've never filled my heart. Only you, hold that honor. You bring joy to my life, a joy I've never known."

"You love me."

"I adore you, baby. I've never loved anyone else." Her heart, which had not beaten in over seven years, exploded with life. She fell into his arms, planting kisses over his face. He grinned. "If I'd known you'd react like this, I would have started a fight long ago." She smiled and continued to shower Dylan with kisses.

Wrapped in each other's arms, they sat in silence until dawn broke over the horizon. The sun's red haze shone against the blue mist of the mountains. Pines created a picturesque arch that slanted into the hillside.

As the first rays of morning slowly ascended, Chrissie perked her ears. A car pulled off the highway and entered the main gate. Immediately, tranquility crashed around them. "Do you hear that?"

"Yes." Dylan tilted his head toward the muffled clatter of a driveshaft. "It sounds like it's close to your car."

"It does, doesn't it?" They listened until the engine died. "Do you think we should check it out?"

"Yeah. We left the keys in the ignition. I didn't expect anyone to be out here at night. "

Chrissie swept the loose hair behind her ear. "Crap!" She stood, her mind swirling with images of her father's reaction.

"No need to panic," Dylan uttered, as he got up. "It's probably the game warden."

"The game warden would drive a truck. That's the sound of a car's engine." Chrissie didn't mind losing her car, but she did dread telling her dad how irresponsible she'd been. He wouldn't be pleased that she spent the night alone with Dylan. This would add insult to injury.

The couple bolted off the hill at top speed. Like two thoroughbreds galloping in a race, they ran neck and neck. When the pair reached the base, they heard the engine roar to life. The tires squealed as the intruder peeled away.

In less than a minute, they inspected the car. Nothing seemed out of place. Nevertheless, when Chrissie opened the door, a familiar scent permeated the interior. As a general rule, she didn't rely on her sense of smell. To clear her nasal passages, she turned her head into the morning air and inhaled. Then, she sniffed the interior of the car. The faint odor of a vampire caused her to recoil. *"Professor Marshall."* She shook her head, to dismiss the notion. *"What would he be doing out here? That's weird. He doesn't smell like a vampire."* After many years of research, Professor Marshall had devised a method of disguising his body odor. However, she could have sworn a trace of his scent lingered in the air. "Do you smell that?"

Without hesitation, Dylan answered, "Yeah, it's a vampire."

Although Chrissie hated it, she allowed a hint of suspicion to flood her thoughts. *"If Dylan can detect the odor of a vampire now, why didn't he recognize my scent when we first met?"* Chrissie scowled. "How do you know?"

"Since I've been around you, I've learned the scent. You each have a different smell, but the same basic fragrance. You smell sweet—like peach blossoms."

Satisfied with his answer, Chrissie focused on the car. While she stroked her chin, she pondered aloud. "Hmm. Why would another vampire be interested in my car?"

"Maybe he recognized the scent, and got curious."

She shrugged. "I guess that makes sense, but it still makes me uncomfortable."

With a sparkle in his eye, Dylan grinned. "Are you ready to go home?"

"Yeah, we've already stayed longer than we should have. Dad's going to be furious."

"No, he won't. He knows you're with me."

Chrissie smirked at his naivety. "Sweetheart. That's the reason he's going to be furious."

Dylan's roared with laughter. The contagiousness of his mirth caused her to snicker. When the jollity died, he beckoned her. "Come here."

With no uncertainty, Chrissie closed the space between them. Dylan caressed her, then pressed his lips against hers. Hot lava flooded her veins, leaving her breathless. She could hear his heart thunder. Running hadn't altered his heart rate, but kissing her caused it to race.

Though Chrissie longed to linger in his arms, she pulled away. "We'd better go."

He rested his forehead against hers. "Alright."

Dylan escorted Chrissie to the passenger's side of the car. He opened the door and held it while she entered. Smiling, she asked, "Will you please get my purse for me?"

"Sure." Once he closed the door, he strolled to the trunk to retrieve her bag.

Suddenly, something aroused Chrissie's defenses. She stared out the side window and scanned the forest for any sign of movement. After, cramming his long limbs into her car, Dylan leisurely propped his left arm over the steering wheel. Before he started the ignition, he glanced at her. "What's wrong?"

"Nothing, I guess." Again, Chrissie scrutinized her surroundings. She couldn't shake the feeling they were being watched.

CHAPTER FOUR
Revelations

Chrissie dropped Dylan off at his apartment before she drove home. She was expecting an onslaught of accusations the moment she opened the door. To her relief, William sat in his office grading papers, seemingly oblivious of her clandestine entrance into the house. Catlike, she crept pass the door to her father's office. As quiet as snow falling on frozen ground, she climbed the backstairs.

Convinced she had pulled off the perfect maneuver, Chrissie twisted her doorknob, then smirked to herself. *"Humph. Who needs to train?"* As soon as she opened the door, she leaped back. Startled, she clutched her chest. "Dad! What are you doing in my room?"

William was perched on the side of her bed. The hems of his black slacks were pulled up, exposing his pale ankles. His white shirt glistened in the moonlit window behind him, making him look like the typical nerdy professor. Seems, she wasn't the only feline in the house.

Though Chrissie hoped he'd failed to hear her surreptitious entrance, such was not the case. *"This was stupid. He probably heard my engine before I turned off the highway."*

Her father's face retained its serenity. "You could've called, Chrissie." Even his grave tone had no hint of anger.

Chrissie removed her zippered hoodie, and then tossed it on the chair in the corner. "Dylan and I needed to talk. We drove to the lake for a little privacy. I didn't want to fight with you, so I just didn't call."

William placed his hand over his mouth. A wide grin graced his lips. Contrary to what she expected, he remained calm. "The next time you and Dylan decide to spend the night out, would you please call me."

"Daddy, I..."

To silence her, William extended his arm, and flattened his palms. "I'm aware that you're old enough to make your own decisions. I also know you can take care of yourself, but I'd still like to know where you are. I'm your father, and I do worry."

Chrissie dropped her keys into her purse. "Since when did you become so understanding?"

He rose from the bed. "Since we had our talk. I promised to trust you, and I thoroughly intend to do so." He inched closer to her. "I may not like all of your decisions. However, I trust you know what's best for you."

Chrissie tossed her purse on the dresser. The mirror provided a clear view of the entire room.

With her back toward William, she watched his every move. "Thanks, Dad, I appreciate your faith in me."

As William straightened his black silk tie, he replied, "I do ask one thing of you…"

Chrissie grimaced. *"Here comes the catch."*

"Please talk to me before you make any major decision about your life. You know, once you do certain things, you can't take them back."

"He sounded like Nana when she wanted to have one of her little woman to woman chats." She turned to face her father. "Dad. You don't need to worry about me. Dylan loves me. He wouldn't do anything to hurt me."

"I loved your mother, too. But, I hurt her." He focused on the gold-framed picture on Chrissie's nightstand. The stunning face of a young, caramel skinned woman stared back. "True. It wasn't my fault." Standing silently, he stared at the photo. "I left her alone, and pregnant with you. I'll have that on my conscience every day for the rest of my existence." He glanced at Chrissie. "Dylan is a warrior. You never know when he'll be called into battle."

Chrissie walked across the room and stood next to him. "To begin…Dylan and I aren't having sex." She took his hand in hers. "Even if we were, I can't get pregnant."

He pulled his hand from hers, and then cleared

his throat. "But therein lays the problem, Peanut. You were born a breeder."

Chrissie scowled. "I'm a what?" She'd never heard the expression in connection to a vampire.

"Most female vampires can't give birth, but you're different. You have the marker."

She gasped. "What marker?"

He stroked his chin, then turn from her view. "You're a breeder, Christina. You ovulate."

"What! Even if that were possible, how would you know?"

"I can smell ovulation as it happens. It has only happened once since your transformation, but it has happened."

Stunned, she sat on the bed. "Daddy. When?"

William sat next to her, his hand tucked beneath his legs. "About a week after you started dating Dylan."

"But, how is that possible?"

"I have no explanation. I only know it's true." He pulled his hands from beneath him, and then ran one over the coral comforter atop the queen-sized bed. "My theory is, because you were ovulating when you were sired, you continued to produce ovum." Grabbing a pillow, he fumbled with the white trim. "Most of our internal organs continue to function as long as we have a blood supply. It isn't unreasonable."

"Daddy." Chrissie widened her eyes in disbelief. "Are you sure?"

"There have been documented cases of active breeders. Why do you think I worry when you're alone with Dylan?" Then, William answered his own question. "I don't want you to end up like your mother."

Chrissie tugged at her ear. "What kind of children can I expect to have?"

William's raised his brows. "Why, vampires, naturally."

"He sounded as if that was the stupidest question he'd ever heard." Her head buzzed with possibilities. "You mean I could have my own children?"

William's joy lit his countenance. "Yes, you can."

When she was transformed, Chrissie abandoned all hope of procreation. The idea of children thrilled her. *"Just think, I can give birth to my own child. That's more than I ever dreamed of."* Her grin exploded. *"Dylan and I could actually have children. I could get used to that."* Absently, she lifted the other pillow and caressed it to her breast. "Dylan and I plan to attend a concert in Bossier tonight. There's an intimate little club called, The Midnight Jam. It features up and coming bands. Tonight, they're featuring bands that cover 80's music."

William patted her hand, then stood. "What time does the show start?"

Dreamy-eyed, Chrissie looked at him. "Bossier is quite a drive. We're going to leave at 6:30. The doors will open at 8:00. We want to get a good table." Radiance lit her face. "I don't mean to rush you, Dad, but I do have homework."

William folded his arms, his hands gripping his biceps.

"What's wrong, Daddy?" William's uncharacteristic nervousness set off Chrissie's alarms.

He cleared his throat again. "Walter, I mean Professor Marshall, asked me to speak to you about something."

Chrissie stiffened. "What? I'm doing well in his class, and Dylan hasn't come into his room since the first day." She pressed her hand against her temple. The subject of Marshall always distressed her. Something about him set her teeth on edge. *"I know he doesn't approve of Dylan. For the life of me, I didn't understand why he seems to hate him."*

William tapped his foot. "Walter would like to visit you."

"Huh?" Chrissie frowned. "Why? What did I do?"

Her father sat back down. "You didn't do anything, Peanut. You don't understand what I'm trying to say."

"What are you trying to say, Dad?"

Before answering, William hesitated. "What I'm trying to say is — he wants to date you."

Astonished, Chrissie's mouth flew open. "Huh? You have got to be kidding." An image of Professor Marshall's face popped into her mind. When she'd processed what her father said, she doubled over in laughter.

At first, William appeared stoic. Yet, the more Chrissie cackled, the wider the grin spread across his face. "Christina. I'm not joking. He wants to date you."

Continuing to laugh, she covered her mouth. "Why in the world would he want to date me?"

William's face hardened. Serious now, he stood. "I told you." Chrissie followed him with her eyes as he lumbered toward the window. "You're a breeder, Peanut." He turned to face her. "He intends to win your affections."

The total import of his comment struck her. The asinine scenario ceased to be funny. Quicker than lightening, she rose. "Are you saying what I think you're saying?"

"If you think I'm saying he wants to marry you, then yes."

Hands on her hips, she yelled, "Are you out of

your mind?"

William recoiled. "Christina, don't raise your voice to me."

"That's positively medieval."

With eyes shut, William took a deep breath. When he spoke, his calm manner had returned. "He really admires you. You're all he talks about when we're alone."

The sheer lunacy of his proposal churned in her mind. *"Marriage. This does explain his animosity toward Dylan."* A black cloud descended upon her mood. "Dad, how could you think I'd even consider something like that? First of all, he's an old man. Secondly, I'm dating Dylan."

William strolled to the dresser. With his hands propped against the top, he explained, "I'm not pushing you in any direction. The choice is yours." He stood straight. "I felt I owed it to you to give you the information. Now, you know you have a choice."

"I thought you had accepted Dylan. How could you think I would even entertain such a notion?"

William moved toward her. "I like Dylan, but you could benefit from Walter's two hundred years of experience."

Livid, she backed away. His rationalization did *not* impress her. "Dylan may not be quite as old, but I love him. That means I don't have a choice."

"I knew you had feelings for him," William mumbled, "but I didn't realize you were in love with him."

"Well now you know, and he loves me. Don't ever ask anything like that of me again."

William headed toward the door, but stopped short. "By the way, how old is Dylan?" His calm demeanor added fuel to the fire that consumed her.

"Why?" she barked.

"He's involved with my daughter. Don't you think I should at least know a little more about him?"

Though Chrissie's anger still smoldered, his reasoning sounded logical. "He's forty-six."

"Is he just beginning college for the first time?"

"This is no time for stupid questions." She shook her head. "No. He first attended college in 93. The warriors summoned him back to the village after the first year."

"I'm curious about something."

"What?"

"He looks to be around nineteen. How long will he live?"

His nonchalant way of questioning refueled her emotional flames. "Why would you ask a question like that?"

"Because, if you're that involved with him, I want to know how many years your relationship is likely to last. Remember, baby, you aren't aging."

Again, his logic quenched the flames. "He's not aging either." She twitched her nose. "Well, not so you'd notice. His people seem to be close to immortal as well. He says his mother is over a hundred, and she still looks twenty."

"If he's not aging, then why does he look like he's in his late teens?"

"From what I understand, once they reach maturity, they age very, very slowly. Other than in battle, Dylan says he has never known any of his people to die."

"Really. That frightens me. He's a warrior, so he can die."

"Don't worry about it. Vampires can be destroyed, too. What's the difference?"

"I just don't want you to get hurt."

"I know, Daddy. If I'm in this world, I can't avoid getting hurt. I'd rather put my heart on the line, than exist without Dylan."

"Humph," William flattened his lips then spoke, "it's gone that far, huh?"

Lips tight, she looked away. "Yeah. It's gone that far."

A sigh escaped William. "Well, I'll leave you

alone now. I'll tell Walter you're not interested." He moved toward the door. Before he crossed the threshold, he stopped then glanced over his shoulder. "I didn't mean to interfere. Walter asked me to mention it to you," he muttered, "and I agreed. Your life is your own. I'll never bring it up again."

"Thanks for understanding."

Placing his hand on the doorframe, he turned. "Do me one favor."

Eyes narrowed, Chrissie grimaced. "What?"

"Take your time. If you two really love each other, you have a long, long time to get to know each other. Don't rush into a physical relationship."

"I won't, Dad." Even as she spoke, she pondered the reality. *"Dylan destroys more and more of my defenses each day. Soon, I won't be able to resist him. How can I talk to my father about something like that?"* She took a deep breath. *"I wish Nana were here."*

CHAPTER FIVE

Reconciled

Class had already started when Chrissie arrived. Self-conscious about Marshall's intentions, she eased into the room. Without calling attention to herself, she slipped into a seat near the back. She occupied her attention by focusing on the worn gold tiles on the floor. Unable to relax, she squirmed in her seat. Each time she looked up, Professor Marshall darted his eyes in another direction. Prior to her class, William must have spoken to him. He ignored her the entire ninety minutes, which was fine with her.

When Marshall dismissed class, Chrissie scrambled to gather her belongings. Anxious to flee the room, she bolted for the door. Before she could execute her escape, Professor Marshall called, "Miss Garrett, may I speak to you for a moment?"

Mortified, Chrissie froze in her tracks. "Yes sir."

Marshall stepped from behind his desk. "I'm going to set up an appointment for you. Tomorrow. My office, at 4:00. We need to talk about your class project."

Her suspicions aroused, she answered, "Yes sir." Without waiting for a response, Chrissie fled the room. Only two other students remained, and she didn't want to be alone with him.

When Chrissie stepped through the doors of Jefferson Hall, she spotted Dylan in his usual place. With legs crossed, he leaned against her car. His usual welcoming smile greeted her. He sported a royal blue t-shirt with a matching cap, turned backwards, of course. As he loped toward her, he questioned, "What took you so long?"

Chrissie constricted her brows and tucked her bottom lip beneath her front teeth. For a fleeting moment, she considered mentioning what her father had told her. Nevertheless, she decided it would cause unnecessary tension between them. "Professor Marshall stopped me."

"Why?" Dylan reached for her backpack. "That drone. What did the old goat want?" Taking potshots at Marshall seemed to please him; he never missed an open opportunity.

Initially, Chrissie feigned a smile, but then she burst into laughter. "He wants to see me in his office tomorrow, at 4:00. It's about my class project."

Slinging her pack over his shoulder, Dylan extended his hand. "Do you want me to go with you?"

Chrissie placed her hand in his. "For what? I've

got this." The couple strolled toward her car.

When they reached the vehicle, Dylan opened the door. He tossed the backpack in the passenger seat. "Do you want me to follow you home? I can wait while you get ready."

"No. It takes only a matter of minutes for me to dress. It'll be faster if you go home. Get dressed, and then pick me up at 6:30."

The corners of Dylan's mouth inched up. His piercing brown eyes twinkled as he leaned against the car. "Come over here."

With no thought to decorum, she rushed into his waiting arms. She pressed her lips against his. Spontaneously, he tightened his grip around her waist. A deep moan erupted from the back of his throat.

When the kiss ended, Chrissie laid her head against his chest. Never had she felt so safe—so complete. "I love you," she murmured. With his index finger, he tilted her chin, then kissed her again. Chrissie felt as if all the love he possessed surrounded her. The world and everyone on it, drifted away. Only she and Dylan remained—two souls, sharing one heart. She locked her arms around his neck, and he lifted her off her feet. Total and complete bliss enfolded her.

Although Chrissie didn't open her eyes, she angled her ears toward the sound of advancing footsteps.

Matt and Estefina were approaching from across the parking lot. Matt snickered under his breath. "Damn. Get a room."

Estefina punched him on the shoulder. "Matt."

Like a little girl, he giggled playfully. "Just sayin."

While ill-advised, Dylan jerked his head in Matt's direction. He shouldn't have been able to hear Matt from that distance, and Chrissie grew concerned. A rumbling sound resonated from deep in his chest. Flashes of green sparked in his deep, brown eyes. Finally, he placed Chrissie on her feet. When Matt and Estefina were within speaking distance, Dylan bristled. "What did you just say?"

With upturned palms, Matt pleaded his case. "It's just a saying, man. No need to get hostile."

In a flash, Dylan swept Chrissie behind him. He advanced toward Matt. "Watch what you say, drone, or you may lose a limb." Dylan towered over Matt, whose five-eleven stature paled in comparison.

Matt recoiled. "Hey. I said, I'm sorry, man. No offense intended." He grabbed Estefina's hand. "I just need to speak with Chrissie."

Standing behind Dylan, Chrissie saw the lengthy muscle in his back as it tensed. With great alacrity, he shifted behind Chrissie, and then slipped his arms around her. "What do you want? Haven't you caused enough trouble?"

Chrissie bumped his abdomen with the back of her elbow. "Behave." She had no desire to speak to Matt ever again. However, out of respect for Estefina, she turned to face him.

Tears glistened in the corners of Estefina's dark eyes. She eased forward, reached for Chrissie's hand, and squeezed it. "I know you're angry with us. You have every right to be, but Matt has something to say. Would you please listen to him — for my sake?"

Her irritation evident, Chrissie wrinkled her nose. "Sure."

Matt crept from behind Estefina. "I'm sorry about last night. I got upset when Estefina and I broke up. Like an idiot, I went out and got drunk." He hung his head. "You know I'm not a drinker. I lost control — said some cruel, mean-spirited things."

Estefina nodded. "I was furious with him last night, too." She touched Chrissie's arm. "This morning when he stopped by my apartment, he was repentant." Estefina squeezed Chrissie's hand. "I decided to forgive him. He didn't even remember what he'd done. When I told him, he felt terrible."

Chrissie detected the inaudible growl emanating from Dylan's chest. She elbowed him with such speed, that neither Estefina, nor Matt would notice.

Although he kept one eye on Dylan, Matt

inched closer. Even through his shirt, Chrissie could see the knots in Dylan's shoulders. "I feel bad, man." Matt continued to focus on Dylan. "I was hurting. I guess I wanted someone else to hurt too. Can we put this behind us? If not for me, do it for Estefina. She and Chrissie are best friends. I don't want her to lose a friend, because I did something stupid."

Chrissie gazed into Estefina's pleading face. A disarming smile brightened her countenance. "Of course, we can put this behind us." She wriggled free of Dylan, and embraced Estefina.

"I'm so sorry." Tears flowed down Estefina's cheeks. "You're the best friend I've ever had. I don't want anything to come between us."

"You have nothing to be sorry about." Chrissie wiped Estefina's tears. "I know you'd never do anything intentionally to hurt me. As for Matt— make him pay for his transgressions later." Chrissie winked, and they both laughed.

Matt extended his hand to Dylan. "Friends?"

Dylan drew back in distaste. If looks could kill, Matt would not only be dead, but also buried six feet under. He glanced at Chrissie, extended his hand, and the two men shook. Once the handshake ended, Dylan rubbed his hand on his jeans.

As though oblivious to Dylan's actions, Matt inquired, "What are you two doing tonight?"

Without thinking, Chrissie blurted out their

plans. "We're going to Midnight Jam. There're three bands playing tonight. It should be awesome."

"I've heard that club is really nice." Estefina gushed. "But I've never been there before. Do you mind if we tag along?"

Pleased about their reunion, Chrissie glowed. "I'd love that."

Dylan rolled his eyes at Chrissie so that no one else noticed. Then, he snarled. "Yeah, that would be great, just great."

Chrissie grimaced. *"Uh oh. This was supposed to be our three month celebration, too late now.*

Matt placed his hand on Dylan's arm. "What time are we leaving, man?"

Jerking to the side, Dylan grumbled, "6:30."

"What?" Matt glimpsed his watch. "It's after 5:30 now." He tugged at Estefina's sleeve. "We'd better hurry."

CHAPTER SIX
The Familiar

Because it could accommodate more people, Dylan drove William's BMW. Estefina and Chrissie sat in the back seat together. They chattered nonstop the entire trip to Bossier. Even though Chrissie had only been angry with Estefina for one day, it seemed like months since they'd spoken. Dylan, however, proved a bit more difficult to mollify. Matt made a feeble attempt at conversation, but Dylan remained cold. Seemingly determined not to enjoy himself, he sat stoic the entire journey.

When they arrived at the club, the parking lot was packed. Dylan circled twice before he found a spot. From the door, the line extended to the parking area. Disappointment engulfed Chrissie. *"Are we too late to get a table?"*

As the group approached the entrance, Matt shoved his hands deep in his pocket. "Man, this place is crowded."

With his arm cuddled around Chrissie's shoulder, Dylan raised a brow. "No joke."

Estefina rubbed her forearms, then bounced up and down. The sun had gone down, and the evening chill had set in. "I'm so cold." She had worn a fitted platinum sequined cocktail dress with a plunging neckline, and matching stilettos. Although she had a wrap, it served more as an accessory than protection against the cold. Before the temperature plummeted, the shawl would have been ideal. As she danced, her teeth chattered. "The weather in this area changes with the blink of an eye. It was seventy-five degrees this afternoon. Now, it feels like it's thirty. I never know how to dress."

Chrissie donned a black and silver brocade cocktail dress with spaghetti straps. A silver jacket completed the outfit. The fitted frock had been designed especially for her. It accentuated her curves to perfection. For obvious reasons, the temperature didn't bother her. She unbuttoned her wrap. "Would you like to borrow my jacket?"

Goosebumps lined Estefina's arms. Her entire body shivered from the cold. Before Chrissie removed her coat, Matt stripped off his leather jacket, and threw it around Estefina's shoulders. "She can wear mine."

Dylan's addition to the night's chill thawed. "I don't think I've ever seen a crowd this large at Midnight Jam before."

Enthralled by the way Dylan's lashes fluttered when he spoke, Chrissie admired him through loving eyes. "Yeah, the band must be good."

To ward off the chill, Estefina pranced from

side to side. "I just hope we get to see them. The doorman turned the last couple away."

At last, Matt pulled Estefina close to him. He draped his arm around her slender shoulders, massaging her arms. "Do you think we should go home or find something else to do?"

"No." Dylan grumbled. One word from Matt seemed to flip his switch. "We're here now. There's only one couple ahead of us, so we may as well wait." He slipped his arm around Chrissie's waist. "Chrissie has been looking forward to this. I don't want to disappoint her."

Though Chrissie detected the anger in Dylan's voice, her lips twitched into a grin. "I don't care what we do, as long as we're together." Nothing pleased her more than having Dylan consider her feelings.

When the doorman turned away the couple in front of them, the group lost all hope of getting inside. Deciding they should probably leave, Chrissie turned to make her suggestion. Suddenly, the attendant pointed at her. "Hey you. What's your name?"

Instinctively, Chrissie stepped back and pointed to herself. "Me?" she muttered. She hesitated before she answered, "I'm Christina. Christina Garrett."

Deep creases etched Dylan's brow; he swept Chrissie behind him. "Why do you need to know?"

The doorman unhinged the purple rope to

allow them entrance, then called to a waiter. "Hey, Joe. Show these folks to their table." Next, he directed his comments to Chrissie. "Your table is ready. You'll be seated down front. Joe will lead the way."

Chrissie tugged Dylan's sleeve, a wide grin resting on her lips. "When did you make reservations?"

Dylan scowled. "I didn't make any reservations."

"Right."

"Really. Chrissie, I didn't make any reservations." He shot Matt a dirty look. "I intended to get here early. I didn't think we'd need one."

Chrissie grew quiet. "Did you make the reservation, Matt?"

"Not me. I didn't know we were coming until 5:30. I wouldn't have had time."

Joe sauntered up to the four. "Follow me." He directed them through the dense crowd, and to the best seats in the house. Below the stage, the center table had been set aside for them. If Chrissie had wanted to, she could've reached out and touch the performers.

Joe, who had obviously overheard the conversation, explained, "The table was reserved by the lead singer of Rolling Thunder."

Dylan glowered "Are you sure we're the right party?"

Joe pulled out a chair to seat Chrissie. "The table is reserved for Christina Garrett, and her party." He pushed the chair beneath her. "All the servers were shown a picture of you. That way we'd be sure we had the right Christina." While Matt assisted Estefina, Dylan seated himself.

Chrissie placed her hand over her heart. "A picture of me?" She leaned her head to one side. Her mannerisms now mirrored Dylan's.

After everyone was seated, Joe turned to leave. "Your server will be with you shortly." With that, he walked away.

Dylan tapered his eyes into slits, simultaneously he flared his nostrils. "Who do you know in Rolling Thunder, Christina?" His voice was firm, yet reserved.

Chrissie heard indignation in his undertone. Calling her Christina always signaled his displeasure. To her relief, the waitress flitted to their table.

"What can I get you?"

Matt ordered for Estefina, and himself. "I'd like two club sodas on the rocks." His bloodshot eyes served as a reminder of the night before.

Dylan held up one finger. "Make that four." Neither he, nor Chrissie drank. Alcohol had no effect on either of them, but they didn't like the effect it had on humans. It slowed their reflexes and clouded their judgment. Matt's performance the previous night had been a prime example.

The waitress scribbled the information on her pad. "Anything else."

Dylan answered for the table. "No. That's all."

The waitress stuck the small black notepad in her apron. On the table, she placed napkins in front of each of them. "I'll be right back with your drinks," she announced before she left.

Dylan interlaced his fingers. Twiddling his thumbs, he said, "You never answered my question, Christina. Who do you know in Rolling Thunder?"

Chrissie rested her elbows on the arm of her chair. "I'm not sure. I've never heard this band before." She shrugged. "I have no clue."

Estefina patted Chrissie's hand. "It has to be someone you know."

Her nerves jangling, Chrissie turned to stare into Estafina's face. "Even so, how would he know I was coming tonight?"

Matt scooted his chair under the table. "You're from California, right?"

Chrissie glared at him. "Yeah. Why?"

"Maybe it's someone you knew out there."

That thought struck a responsive chord. Chrissie did know a singer from California. As a matter-of-fact, she had discussed the same singer with Dylan the night before — Jayden Ballenger. She stroked her chin. *"Surely, Jay wouldn't be the lead singer of this band. The last time we talked, he sang with a band called Starlight."* With a tilt of her head, she glanced at Matt. "I knew some singers out there. Even so, I still wonder how he'd know I'd be here tonight."

Dylan leaned forward in his seat. "Good question. How would he know you were going to be here tonight?"

At that moment, the waitress returned with their order. The young woman set a drink before each of them. Chrissie was grateful for the brief reprieve. No sooner than the server strolled away, the opening band paraded out. The first two bands gave mediocre performances. They lacked the pizzazz Chrissie had anticipated.

That feeling changed when Rolling Thunder took the stage. While the curtains opened, the pianist played an unfamiliar tune. As the bassist strolled to his position at right center stage, he added the rhythm. The lead-guitarist followed, taking his place at left center stage. Back-up singers marched out last. They took their spots upstage left. Multicolored lights blinded the audience, while the overhead lights went down. When they rose again, the lead-singer stood center stage with his back to the crowd.

Without a glimpse of his features, Chrissie recognized the star performer. The familiar scent of his shoulder-length black hair filled her nostrils. He stood six feet tall, with a flawless physique, and his tailored suit accentuated the width of his board chest. Ladies in the audience screamed at the sight of him.

Jayden gyrated with the music, and his fragrance permeated the room. Chrissie's mouth watered at the memory of his flavor. She swept her hair behind her ear, and her eyes flickered. The assault on her senses left her mesmerized. Without thinking, she murmured, "Jay."

Obviously hearing her blunder, Dylan's turned sharply. A soft rumble reverberated in his chest.

Before he faced the audience, Jayden, an angelic tenor, began to sing. His voice rolled from his tongue effortlessly, as he moved from tenor to bass. The band's performance rivaled any Chrissie had ever seen.

Dylan situated his chair close enough to sit with his arms around Chrissie's shoulders. Though it took a while, he seemed to relax. Then, the band keyed up "Our Love Will Never Die," an original song Jay had composed. As he sang, Jayden sauntered off stage and over to their table. Extending his hand, he reached for Chrissie's. Unsure how to react, she followed him as he sang, "Two hearts always so true. I loved her, and she loved me too." As he led her up the stairs, he hit every note with precision.

Once Chrissie hit the platform, Jayden caressed her face. While he gazed deeply into her eyes, he crooned lyrics that spoke of undying love. When he finished his last note, he leaned in until his lips pressed against hers. The audience exploded. From the stage, Chrissie caught a glimpse of Dylan's eyes. There, she spied splashes of green against a bed of white. Their gorgeous brown hue had been obliterated by jealousy. Now, his features resembled something other-worldly.

Seeing Dylan's reaction, Chrissie went into full panic mode. As soon as Jayden released her, she rushed from the stage. Unfortunately, he had not finished twisting the proverbial knife. For his final selection, he chose "She's My Girl," another original compositions. When he crooned, he pointed his finger at Chrissie. The lyrics indicated that she had broken his heart.

Once again, Jayden strolled off the stage. This time, he stood directly over Chrissie, touched her face, and continued his serenade. Though his rendition was exceptional, her desire for him to finish was undeniable. To add insult to injury, he pointed at Dylan. Jay sang words which seemed specifically aimed at injuring Dylan's pride. "You're with her now. That fact I can't deny, but I'll get her back some way, somehow."

Chrissie's mind swirled. *"Has Jay been listening to our conversations? How could he have known which songs would exact the most pain?"*

With one hand, Dylan clenched the leg of his

chair with such force Chrissie thought it would crumble beneath his strength. Though she didn't see him, she heard what sounded like claws grating against metal. There was no way Estefina and Matt missed the growls that erupted from him. She nodded toward the stage, non-verbally communicating to Jay. For his safety, he needed to leave. Instead, he lifted her hand and kissed it.

After what seemed an eternity, Jay shared his attention with the rest of the audience. With a wink at Estefina, he strutted around to her side of the table, then squeezed her hand. When the guitar solo began, Jayden flitted through the audience. A true entertainer, he showered squealing ladies with hugs and kisses. As he began the final chorus, Jayden returned to the stage. The audience leaped to their feet in applause. His theatrics ended none too soon, leaving Chrissie mortified.

Hand over heart, Estefina sank into her chair. "Chrissie, do you know him?"

Initially unable to speak, Chrissie swallowed the lump in her throat. "Yes. I knew him in California."

As she clutched Chrissie's wrist, Estefina prattled. "He is *so* hot."

With an air of indifference, Chrissie responded, "I guess." Her one goal was to placate Dylan's anger.

Dylan placed his knotted hands atop the table.

"Who is he, *Christina*?"

Chrissie's brain was abuzz with activity. *"Uh oh. I'm in deeep trouble."* She bit her lip before she answered. "He's Jayden Ballenger. You remember. We've talked about him before. He's the guy we talked about yesterday."

He picked up his drink. The clear liquid swirled in the glass. "Isn't it interesting you tell me about him one day, and he serenades you the next?" His serene tone frightened her.

Chrissie wrapped her hand around his, and lowered the glass. "Purely coincidental."

The tension was already palpable between the couple when the server strolled over to the table. She leaned close to Chrissie's ear. "Are you Christina Garrett?"

"Oh, no. What now" Chrissie stammered, "Y, yes." If she had been able to perspire, streams of water would have flowed onto the floor.

From her apron pocket, the waitress retrieved a note. "Jayden Ballenger, the lead singer of Rolling Thunder, asked me to give this to you."

The young woman handed the note to Chrissie. Afraid of Dylan's reaction, Chrissie crushed the letter in her palm. "I know him. Thanks."

Grinning, the server patted Chrissie on the shoulder. "You're so lucky. I've been trying to get next to him since he got here. I wondered about him until I saw him look at you." Head tilted, she inhaled. "*Girl*. What I wouldn't give to have a man gaze at me like that." With lips parted, her mouth looked as if she would drool at any moment.

Dylan grasped the arm of his chair. Chrissie attuned her ears to the crackle of splintering wood. Too afraid to look, she cut her eyes in his direction. She had a sick feeling that before they left, they would be forced to pay for damages.

As the waitress swished away, Chrissie mumbled, "Thanks." She opened her purse to shove the letter inside.

Dylan, however, had other ideas. "Read the note, Christina." The green glint in his eyes revealed his fury; however, his voice remained calm. "Aren't you curious to find out what he wants?"

Enough had happened that day, and more trouble was the last thing Chrissie wanted. She glanced at the envelope marked *urgent*. Reluctantly, she tore it open.

Hi Chrissie,

After the show, I need to talk to you about something very important. I'll be off stage by one, so meet me backstage at 1:15.

Love you, Jay

While Chrissie read the note, she felt Dylan's gaze burn into her. After she finished, he extended his hand. With her throat constricting, she eased the letter into his palm. In less than four seconds, he digested the contents. "Are you going to meet him?"

Chrissie squirmed in her seat. "I hadn't planned to."

Digging in her purse, Estefina retrieved a tissue. The cold air had left her with a sniffle. "I think you should." She wiped her nose. "It would be rude to ignore an old friend. Where do you know him from anyway?"

Before Chrissie responded, she lifted her glass. "I've known him since I was ten." She took a sip of the watery club soda. "We grew up next door to each other."

Quick to mimic Chrissie, Estefina sipped her drink. As she lowered the glass, the ice clinked against the side. "Has he always had a case for you?"

Still aware of Dylan's anger, Chrissie snatched a quick glimpse in his direction. His scowl confirmed her suspicions. "What do you mean?"

Estefina scooted to the edge of her chair. "Do you mind if I go backstage with you?"

The biceps beneath Dylan's shirt bulged when he folded his arms. "Yes, Christina, why don't we *all* go backstage with you? I'm sure Jayden won't mind since you and he are so close." Acid spewed from each syllable.

Outnumbered, Chrissie acquiesced. "Okay." She dreaded the impending catastrophe.

* * * * *

All four made their way to the corridor, leading to the dressing rooms. Arms crossed, an enormous bouncer stood like a Roman centurion, blocking the entrance to Jayden's dressing room. "No one's allowed beyond this point without a pass." The average person would have been intimidated by his imposing physique. Yet, he posed no threat to Dylan, or Chrissie either for that matter.

Before Chrissie could offer an explanation, Jayden opened his door, then bolted from his dressing room. He wrapped her in a bear hug and hoisted her into the air. As though she were weightless, he spun her like a rag doll. "Hey, Chrissie, I've missed you so much. It's good to see you. You look great." Brimming with excitement, all of Jay's sentences blended together. He set her on her heels, shook his head, and then stared at her for a few seconds.

Chrissie pointed to each person while she made her introductions. "Jayden Ballenger, I'd like you to meet my friends. That's Estefina Garcia, her boyfriend, Matthew Jenkins, and this is my boyfriend, Dylan Duncan."

With an edge of contempt, Jayden repeated, "Your boyfriend. Humph." He ogled Dylan from head to toe. "No wonder you looked so pissed when I sang to Chrissie. Sorry about that, dude."

His muscles stiff, Dylan responded, "No offense taken."

Convinced Dylan had lied through his teeth, Chrissie stepped slightly in front of him. She didn't want to chance a confrontation. "What do you want to talk to me about?"

As he led the way into the dressing room, Jayden answered, "Let me introduce your friends to the guys. They can sit in here while we talk." Once inside the dressing room, Jayden made the introductions. "Guys, this is Estefina, Matthew, and Dylan." He pointed to Chrissie separately. "And this is Christina, Christina Garrett. We grew up together."

Matthew extended his hand. "Call me Matt."

"They're going to visit with you while I talk with Chrissie." Dylan frowned, but said nothing.

Estefina and Matt sat on the couch while Dylan remained rigid. He placed his arm around Chrissie's back.

Jayden continued to scrutinize Dylan, scanning the full length of his body. "Why don't you have a seat? Relax while Chrissie and I visit?"

Her mind racing, Chrissie pursed her lips. *"That isn't going to fly."*

Dylan pulled her closer to him. "I'll stay with Chrissie if you don't mind."

Glaring at Dylan, Jayden shrugged. "Suit yourself." He led the way to the instrument room.

No sooner had the door shut, than Chrissie asked again, "So. What's up, Jay?"

Jayden didn't reply. Instead, he addressed Dylan. "Are *you* her *new* familiar?"

Dylan tensed his arm around Chrissie's waist. "I'm extremely familiar with Chrissie, but not the way you think." To show ownership, he kissed her neck.

Chrissie held her breath in apprehension. Her first love, and the man she adored, stood face to face. She couldn't think of a more dangerous scenario.

The red margins of Jayden's lips narrowed. All aspects of his face crinkled in the middle. "Is that a fact?"

"That's a fact." Dylan stepped forward. "You got a problem with it?" Chrissie had only seen Dylan that hostile once. The altercation with her father and Professor Marshall had brought out the worst in him.

Though Jayden stood three inches shorter than Dylan, he advanced. "You're not a vampire. You're *not* human. What are you?"

Chrissie's face grew ashen. *"He noticed something in Dylan I missed when I first met him. But then, he isn't romantically attracted to him."*

Seemingly to demonstrate his absolute victory over Jayden, Dylan kissed Chrissie's neck again. "I'm the man she loves."

Jayden scowled. "You use the term *man* loosely don't you? You're not a man."

Dylan released Chrissie. With his left arm, he maneuvered her behind him. "When your face kisses that floor, it won't matter what I am." He glowered. "I guarantee you won't be able to get up by yourself."

"Really," Jayden retorted, stepping forward. "I don't see your boys. Are they hiding behind you? Brave man."

"Don't antagonize me. If I hit you, they'll still be searching for your pieces, next week."

Before testosterone could rise higher, Chrissie interceded. "Enough guys." Arms spread, she moved between them. "Why are you here, Jay? I told you to stay and watch Nana."

Still sizing up Dylan, Jayden's voice resonated, "It's about your grandmother." Although he spoke to Chrissie, he locked eyes with his target.

Hearing Nana's name Chrissie moved closer to Jayden, but Dylan caught her wrist. "What about Nana?"

"She disappeared about a month ago."

"What?" Chrissie strained to break Dylan's

grip. "Why didn't you contact me?"

With arms at his side, Jayden uplifted palms. "How was I supposed to contact you? Before you left, you changed your phone number. Maybe I'm mistaken, but I don't recall your giving it to me. You didn't tell me where you were going. All I knew was that you were headed for Texas. I've been looking for you for months, even before your grandmother's disappearance. That's why I joined the band. I knew you were a fan of 80's music. We tour all the major cities—Dallas, Fort Worth, and Houston. I hoped you would come to one of our shows. I reserve a table in your name, at every engagement."

"Okay, okay." Chrissie waved her hands before her face then rested them on her cheeks. "Wh, what happened to Nana?" She shook with hysteria. Her grandmother had raised her from the time her mom died. No one had ever been closer to her, not even her dad.

"I don't know. When I went to check on her, she wasn't there. I waited, but she never came back."

With knees apart, Dylan lowered his body in an aggressive stance. "Did you call the police?"

Jayden turned bright red. "Of course, I did. I waited a few hours, and then I called."

"Jay. Why weren't you watching her like I told you?" Chrissie wasn't really angry with Jayden. She was angry with herself for leaving.

"I couldn't watch her every minute. I was hanging around so much she was getting suspicious. As it was, she told me to get a life. She suspected I hung around her because I missed you so much."

Dylan reached for Chrissie's hand, then squeezed it. "What do you want to do?"

Without hesitation, she answered, "I need to speak to my dad."

Jayden eased toward her. "What do you need me to do?"

Dylan clutched Chrissie to him. He angled his body so Jayden couldn't touch her. "You've done enough. She doesn't need you to do anything else."

Though Jayden hadn't been transformed, he crouched and bared his teeth. "I don't recall saying anything to you."

Before the squabble digressed into a full-fledged fight, Chrissie grabbed Dylan's arm. Though physically not in his league, she was strong enough to restrain him. "For the moment, stay on tour. If I need you, I'll send for you. Do you have a copy of your itinerary?"

"Yeah. I've got one in my pocket.

Chrissie reached around Dylan. "Give it to me."

Jayden dug into his pocket and then pulled out a copy of his tour dates. "When will I see you again?" His tone reflected his pain.

Chrissie's heart melted. "I don't know, Jay." As a general rule, a familiar does everything with the vampire who initiated him. With no regard for the suffering she would cause him, Chrissie had left Jayden behind. He hadn't seen her in several months. Like all familiars, he longed for her as much as she did for him. "I'll send for you, *if* I need you." While she regretted leaving, she released her familiar. "We've got to go." Nothing was more important to her than Dylan, not even the first man who kissed her.

"I've missed you every day, Chrissie. Life just isn't the same without you."

"I know. I miss you too, Jay." Dylan made no comment. He didn't need to. The tortured expression on his face spoke volumes.

Once Chrissie's conversation with Jay ended, she heard Estefina's comments streaming down the hall from the dressing room. "You should be ashamed of yourself, Matt. Chrissie and Dylan are our friends."

"What?" he responded.

"How dare you talk about them behind their backs!" Estefina's voice echoed with anger.

Jayden led the way back to the dressing room. As their footsteps clicked against the hardwood floor, the chatting ceased. Chrissie wondered what had been said that caused Estefina's ire. Normally, she would have listened to the discussion, but she had been so preoccupied with her grandmother that she missed their interaction.

When they entered the room, Dylan took charge. "Let's go guys. We've got to roll."

Like any small child, Matt whined. "Man. What's the hurry?"

The veins in Dylan's square jaws contracted. "If you don't want to hitch a ride back home, you'd better get a move on." Without another word, he reached for Chrissie's hand, and marched toward the door.

"Dylan," Estefina called, "do we have enough time for me to go to the powder room?"

Stopping in mid-step, Dylan turned. "Make it quick. We need to leave as soon as possible." Matt glanced over at Gary and rolled his eyes.

"I'll hurry," Estefina replied, as she stepped forward and grabbed Chrissie's hand. "Come with me. You know I hate to go to the ladies' room alone." Before Chrissie could answer, Estefina practically dragged her down the hallway.

Pointing to the restroom in the lounge, Kyle said, "Ladies, there's a restroom right there."

"I know," Estefina answered, "but that's for you guys. I prefer using the one in the hall."

Matt chuckled. "For the life of me, I can't figure

out why women go to the bathroom together. If men did that, people would think they were weird."

Estefina grumbled, "Shut up, Matt."

When the ladies entered the powder room, Estefina stopped, and then stared at the floor for several seconds. Confused, Chrissie commented, "I thought you had to use the facilities."

Shaking her head, Estefina moved close to her friend. "There's something I feel I should tell you, but I don't know…"

"What?" Chrissie raised her hands in a question. "What is it?"

Estefina walked to the sink. "I don't want to cause trouble."

"If it concerns me, I need to know."

Estefina rested her posterior against the sink, bit her lip, and then recounted what transpired in Chrissie's absence.

"At first, we were having a nice time. Then Matt sat on the couch with a malicious grin on his face. I've known Matt forever, Chrissie. I know when he's about to screw up. Everything was just perfect, then Matt said, "That guy is really feeling Chrissie, isn't he?"

Kyle was placing his bass guitar in its case, then he snaps the latch and says, "Always." He walked across the room to the sofa, and then sat down next to me.

Now, Gary seemed a bit more sincere than the others. "Yeah," he says, "Jay talks about her non-stop. I thought she was a figment of his imagination until tonight."

Kyle set his case next to Gary's guitar. After that, *he* joined the conversation. "No joke. Now that I've seen her, I can understand why he's so sprung."

Unaware of her stance, Estefina folded her arms in Chrissie defense. "Then this Brad character struts into the room from the shower, wet hair and all. And he's wearing only a towel. I couldn't believe it—he plops into the chair opposite me. "Now, she is fine," he says, while he dries his hair. Had the nerve to ask, "What's going on with that weird guy she's with?"

At that time, Matt seized the opportunity to take a stab at Dylan. "Ah, he's full of himself—thinks he owns her," he says.

I was furious. You know Matt has a big mouth, so I poked him in the ribs to make him shut up. "They're a couple, you idiot. You know how crazy they are about each other."

Sometimes I swear Matt has rocks for brains. He says, "Well, it seems to me, that if Jayden has his way, they won't be a couple for very long."

Blinking her eyes, Estefina seemed to wake from a long sleep. "Well. That's what happened. I started not to tell you. But, I didn't want a recurrence of the Kaylee incident."

"I'm glad you did." Chrissie shrugged. "It's not a big deal. Still, I preferred to know." With that, the ladies returned to the dressing room. Chrissie wondered how Dylan would react to this new revelation. With his keen ear, he was sure to have heard their conversation. She grimaced at the notion. *"If the circumstances were reversed, it would bother me."*

Dylan was perched against the door, waiting when Chrissie got back to the lounge. "Ready?" Chrissie nodded, and the couple headed for the exit.

Clearly, upset, Estefina barked from the hall. "Let's go, Matt." Matt eased out of his seat, then trailed the others.

Before the group crossed the threshold, Jayden called, "Chrissie."

Chrissie stopped cold, and then faced him. "What is it, Jay?"

"I need you." He hesitated for a second. "You know what I mean." Dylan turned sharply? A vicious growl escaped his lips. Every mouth in the room dropped open, except Jay's.

Afraid of what Dylan had made of that statement, Chrissie swallowed hard, and then reestablished her mental connection with Jay. *"I know."* A familiar could survive without the vampire who initiated him, but it was difficult.

Once a human was bitten, he yearned to repeat the euphoric sensation. The experience resembled an addict craving a powerful drug.

Jayden ran his hand through his silky mane, still damp from his performance. *"I can't wait much longer. It's been so long since the last time."*

Though Chrissie realized Dylan would question why she and Jay had made eye contact for so long, she continued to gaze at him. *"I'll take care of it. I promise."*

"We'll be here for two more days. Can I depend on you before I go?"

"I said I would. Didn't I?"

Jay tilted his head toward Dylan. *"What about him? Will he let you out of his sight, or does he understand our relationship?"*

Chrissie peeked at Dylan, whose chest expanded and contracted in rapid succession. Then, she looked at Jayden. "Call me tomorrow. My new cell phone number is 555 333-0011." When Dylan tightened his iron grip on her wrist, she cringed.

With his voice barely audible, Jayden confessed. "Seriously. I've really missed you."

Chrissie yearned to comfort him. However, what Chrissie needed to do required privacy; not even Dylan could witness their interaction. "I know. Me too. I'll talk to you tomorrow."

Not allowing Jay another remark, Dylan stormed through the door with Chrissie in tow.

CHAPTER SEVEN

Bitter Dregs

During the trip home, tension flooded the car. While Dylan sulked, Estefina chastised Matt for his crude comments about Jay and Chrissie. Dylan only spoke when he couldn't avoid it. However, Chrissie was too overwrought to care what transpired around her. She heard background voices, but didn't realize they were directed at her.

Estefina called, "Chrissie." But Chrissie didn't respond. An impenetrable cloud of fear had enveloped her brain, leaving no room for trivial matters. "Chrissie!" When the fog lifted, Chrissie jumped. Everyone in the car stared in her direction. "Where were you?"

Chrissie shook her head to clear the mist. "I'm sorry. I was thinking. Did you say something?"

Estefina placed her hand on Chrissie's shoulder. "I said I'm sorry about what happened tonight."

Chrissie blinked several times. "Huh? What are you sorry about? What did you do?" Her concern for Nana prevented her from processing Estefina's apology.

Dylan glared. His demeanor echoed his displeasure with everyone. "I believe Estefina means the comments Matt made about you and Jayden while we were at the club."

Leaning forward, Matt put his hand on the back of Dylan's seat. "This is the second time I've had to say this tonight, but I'm sorry. Sometimes, I open my big mouth before I think about what I'm saying."

Estefina punched his arm. "Sometimes."

"Okay. Okay. I do it a lot."

Chrissie tilted her head toward the back seat. "It's alright. You just got carried away."

Dylan gritted his teeth and fired, unleashing the full extent of his rage. "It's *not* okay. That's the second time, in two days, you've interfered in our relationship. If you plan to get any older, don't do it again."

"Dylan." Chrissie intervened. "Don't be rude."

Emerald flashed in Dylan's brown eyes. "I'll do more than be rude if the little drone does it again."

Matt cowered in the backseat. "I—I'm really sorry, man."

Before she faced the back, Chrissie glared at Dylan for a moment. "It's okay, Matt. Dylan is just jealous, and taking it out on you."

Tightly clutching the steering wheel, Dylan

vented, "Don't apologize for me. I have every right to be jealous. Jayden is delusional. He's lucky I didn't remove his spleen."

Estefina gasped, and then covered her mouth. The whites of Matt's eyes reflected the moonlight shining through the window. His face ashened; he appeared frightened out of his wits.

Chrissie turned to face Dylan. "Let's not discuss this, now. We'll talk when we get home."

"They witnessed Jayden flirting with you. Why should we hide our conversation?" Dylan refused to let it go. He was usually easy going and willing to forgive. This time, he seemed determined to start a fight.

"What's wrong with you, Dylan? You've been nursing a serious attitude all evening."

His chest heaving in anger, Dylan turned to face Chrissie. The seat belt cut into his neck as he grumbled. "You have to ask me why I'm upset. Where have you been all night?"

"I know Jay did some things that upset you, Chrissie sighed, but they were just a part of his act."

Dylan's features contorted into something unrecognizable. "He put his hands on you."

"Seriously, Dylan, it didn't mean anything. I told you, it's a part of his act."

"It may not have meant anything to you, but I

saw the way he looked at you. He's in love with you."

"Let's not have this conversation now. If you still want to talk when we get home, we'll finish it then."

"We're going to talk about this now." He smashed his fist into the dashboard. "That man's in love with you."

Chrissie shook her head. "I can't help that, Dylan."

"You didn't do anything to discourage it. 'I've missed you, too.'" Dylan used her words as a weapon against her.

A cruel streak rose inside Chrissie, and she blurted the truth. "Well, I have missed him. Jay's been a loyal friend to me. I'd think, you of all people, would appreciate that."

Clenching his teeth, Dylan asked, "What did he mean when he said, *he needed you?*"

Although infuriated, Chrissie decided to be the voice of reason. Before she spoke, she softened her tone. "Dylan, I can't talk about this right now." Using her peripheral vision, she glimpsed her friends. "It's complicated."

Without warning, Dylan blasted her. "Did you sleep with him?"

Too furious to speak, Chrissie glared at Dylan. "How dare you ask me a question like that?"

"Answer the question, Christina. Did you have sex with that man?"

"First of all," Chrissie growled, "that's none of your business. Secondly, I *refuse* to dignify that with an answer."

Dylan took his eyes off the road, and then removed one hand from the wheel. He raised his finger. "Either you're going to tell me the truth, or I'll go back to that club and beat the answer out of Jayden."

"We talked about this last night." Chrissie braced her hand against the dash. "I told you I had never been with anyone else. Besides, you said whatever we did before we got together was irrelevant. Does that only apply to you?" From the corner of her eyes, Chrissie noticed Matt was nodding his head.

All aspects of Dylan's face crinkled. The downy fuzz along his hairline bristled with indignation. "I told you the truth. I admitted I would change certain things if I could, but you pretended to be so innocent. Why did you lie to me?"

Steely eyed, Chrissie glared at Dylan. "I didn't lie to you. There hasn't been anyone else in my life. Before I met you, I never even considered being with anyone. Why can't you accept that?"

Dylan's baritone voice resonated, "Because, he put his hands on you." Waves of disapproval distorted his countenance.

The strain of the evening crashed down on Chrissie. Trembling all over, she closed her eyes. "Stop it, Dylan. Just stop it. I can't fight with you right now. I don't have the energy." She rubbed her temples. "Take me home." Tears welled in her eyes, but they didn't fall.

When Dylan glanced at Chrissie, the scowl that had once marred his features melted. He pulled off the road and parked. After he exited the car, he walked to the passenger side, then opened the door. Reaching for Chrissie's hand, he helped her out.

Without taking his eyes off Chrissie, Dylan informed their companions. "We'll be right back." Although he sounded tranquil, concern remained imprinted on Estefina's face.

Dylan held Chrissie's hand as he led her a short distance from the car. Once the couple walked far enough so Matt and Estefina couldn't hear, Dylan placed a gentle palm against her cheek. "Chrissie, I love you. I know I'm overreacting, but it killed me to see another man touch you. You're right, though. This is no time for me to put additional stress on you." He pulled her into his arms and kissed her hair. "I'm so sorry. I've been acting like such a jerk all evening."

Chrissie buried her head in his chest. "I know this hasn't been the best night of our lives, but I need your support." She inhaled and expelled the air. "I love you, too. I'm sorry Jay pulled his little stunt tonight. I really didn't know he would be there. If I had, I would've warned you."

"Don't worry about that. We need to concentrate on finding out what happened to your grandmother. That's all that matters right now — making sure she's safe."

"Thank you," she whispered. "I need you with me. I can't face this without you."

Using his index finger, he tilted her chin. "You'll never have to face anything without me. I promise."

As they strolled back to the car, Chrissie overheard Matt. "You see. If she wasn't having sex with Dylan, she wouldn't have said, '*I haven't been with anyone else.*' Why do you think he's so jealous? A man doesn't get that jealous of someone he's not sleeping with. You're the only one still holding out."

Chrissie resented Matt for conveniently misusing her words to pressure her friend. She didn't know when she would do it, but she had to explain what she meant.

CHAPTER EIGHT
Preparations

Dylan parked William's car in its usual spot. As Chrissie opened the car door, she called, "Dad." She never raised her voice. In her world, increased volume wasn't necessary. Both her father and Dylan could hear an ant crawling over wet grass.

Before she shut the door, William stood next to her, his forehead creased. "What's wrong, Chrissie?"

She sprinted into her father's arms. "Nana's missing, Daddy, and I don't know what to do. I don't know where to start."

William draped his arm around her shoulder. "Take a breath, Peanut." He scrutinized her haggard face. "Let's go into the house and sit down. Tell me exactly what happened."

The threesome marched into the family room. Dylan and Chrissie sat together on the love seat. Distraught, she clung to him for moral support. If he had been human, his hand would have crumpled beneath the pressure of her grip. As calmly as she could manage, she repeated everything Jayden had told her.

William listened, stroking his chin while Chrissie babbled. If he were alarmed, his demeanor never gave away his apprehension. "The first thing we need to do is verify the facts. I'll call the Pinole Police Department. They may have found her by now."

Chrissie sprang forward in her seat. "But Jay said..."

"I know what Jayden told you," William interrupted, "but let's make sure."

Dylan, who had remained silent, agreed. "Your dad is right, Chrissie. You may be getting upset unnecessarily." He wrapped his arm around her.

Although Chrissie didn't want to waste time with the police, she consented to wait. William rose and went to his office. She attempted to follow, but Dylan restrained her. While William googled the Pinole Police Department to attain the phone number, she sat on the edge of the seat.

"Calm down, sweetheart," Dylan said, as he stroked her hand. But, she was beyond being placated.

Sitting in his office, William reached into his pocket to retrieve his cell. He dialed the numbers too fast for Chrissie to discern the digits. A short interval followed, and then he spoke. "Yes. This is Professor William Garrett. I'm calling in reference to Mrs. Rebecca Scott." A brief pause ensued before William continued. "She is my late daughter's grandmother." Chrissie had never heard herself referred to as *late*; the concept unsettled her. "I heard she disappeared from her home. I'm wondering if these rumors were true." Another short interval passed. "I see. So there's been no trace of her since?" Silence. Chrissie held her breath in trepidation. "I'll give you my phone number. If you learn anything else, or if she turns up, would you please give me a call?"

Chrissie glanced up when William's cell phone click off. An instant later he reappeared.

As she jumped to her feet, Chrissie asked, "What did they say?" Within seconds, Dylan stood behind her, enfolding her in his arms.

"It's true." William laid his hand atop his daughter's. "Your grandmother disappeared four weeks ago and hasn't been seen since. No sign of a struggle existed inside the house. Yet, the garage door had been torn from it hinges." He bit the inside of his jaw. "Her assailants replaced the door."

Dylan tightened his grip on Chrissie's waist. "It sounds as though this kidnapping was the work of amateurs."

While he tapped his index finger against his lip, William speculated. "Yes. And it doesn't sound like the work of a human. He said the door was torn off its hinges. Someone exceedingly strong perpetrated this."

Past anxious, Chrissie shuddered. "Who would want to kidnap Nana? And why? She doesn't have anything to speak of."

William strolled to the fireplace. Staring at the bricks, he mused aloud. "There has to be some motive—some reason behind this. Something we don't see."

As he listened, Dylan formulated his own plan. "No one asked me, but I think we should go down there—check it out for ourselves."

"I think you're right." William walked to the couple. He placed his hand on Dylan's shoulder. "How long will it take you to pack?"

"I can be back in half an hour." Dylan kissed the top of Chrissie's head. Using long strides, he headed for the door.

"Great. I'll make arrangements for a flight while you're gone." William was already searching the phone book for the airport's number.

Chrissie trailed Dylan to the door. When he reached the threshold, he pulled her near. "I'll be back as soon as I can. Try not to worry. We'll find your grandmother."

Feigning a smile, Chrissie kissed his cheek. It took a couple of seconds for his statement to soak in. When Chrissie realized what he had said, she pushed him away. "What do you mean—we.

A look of bewilderment spread across Dylan's

face. "Just that. We'll find her."

Chrissie folded her arms tightly across her chest. "Are you speaking of you and dad?"

Confused, he shrugged. "Yes. Who else?"

"Where do you think I'll be while you track down my nana?"

"You're going to wait here."

With fears lifted, rage raced through Chrissie. "Have you lost your mind? Do you really think you're going to leave me at home while you fly across the country in search of *my grandmother*?"

From behind her in the family room, Chrissie heard William say, "You really should stay here, Chrissie. There's nothing you can do anyway."

"There's nothing I can do here either." She turned to face the family room. "I'm going."

This time, Dylan grabbed her wrist, and spun her around. "You aren't going. That's final."

Chrissie bared her fangs, and pulled away. "You're not my husband, and you're not my father. You have no right to tell me what to do."

Turning on his heels, Dylan marched out the door. "I don't have time to discuss this, right now. We'll talk about it later." Chrissie stared after him. When he reached the end of the sidewalk, he stopped then hesitated for several seconds. Looking over his shoulder, he glanced at her. "By the way, I love you." Now, his voice was serene. "Everything will be alright."

"I love you too." Chrissie eased the door shut. When she turned, she was startled by her dad, who stood directly behind her. She placed her hand over her heart. "How do you do that?" It never ceased to amaze her how stealthily her dad slinked into a room. His movement was so clandestine, that even her keen hearing didn't discern him.

William ignored her question. "You really should stay here."

"How can you ask me to stay here, when Nana may be in danger? If you find her, she won't know you."

"That's just the point. Have you considered what may happen if she sees you? You *are* supposed to be dead you know."

She grimaced in repulsion. "I hadn't thought about that."

"Well, think about it, baby." He lowered his gaze. "I made a choice for you. Now, you're paying the cost for my decision."

"What are you talking about, Dad?"

"You know what I mean. Because of my selfishness, you must face eternity neither alive nor dead."

"Poor Daddy. I never realized how guilty he felt

about transforming me." Chrissie hooked her arm through William's. The pair strolled toward the den. "Dad, you did what you had to do." She stopped and stared into his eyes. "I don't regret your decision. I have you and Dylan. I couldn't be happier."

With his head hung, William lamented. "You don't have to say that for my benefit."

"I'm not saying it to make you feel better. If you hadn't had the courage to sire me, I would have died without knowing you. What's more, I never would have met Dylan." This time, it was Chrissie who lifted his chin. "The two of you are the most important people in my world." She grinned. "I wouldn't change that for anything." William forced a weak smile, but Chrissie realized he still felt awful. "May I ask you something?"

William sat down in his recliner. "What?"

Chrissie sat on the arm of the chair next to him. "Do you regret changing me?"

He turned his head in her direction. "No. Not at all. There isn't a day that goes by that I'm not thankful that you're with me."

"I feel the same way. If we're both grateful that we're together, what's the problem?"

With a twinkle in his eyes, William chortled. "You have a point." Patting her leg, he relented. "Well, if we're going to be ready when Dylan returns, we'd better pack."

CHAPTER NINE
Nana's

During the drive to the airport, William tried to lift Chrissie's spirits by discussing their summer plans. She, however, refused to be comforted. Dylan grumbled each time William made a comment. His displeasure for her refusal to stay home was apparent, but she hardly noticed. Her grandmother's safety pervaded her every thought. She couldn't sit idly by while someone else attempted to rescue her nana.

The flight didn't leave until 6 a.m., but the threesome arrived at 3:30. William had suggested they wait a little longer before heading out, but Chrissie was too antsy. Boarding finally began at 5:30. Because they were flying first class, the small group preceded the others onto the plane. Dylan sat next to Chrissie while her dad sat directly behind her. A bald, heavy set man occupied the seat next to William.

Once they settled into their seats, a short time passed before Dylan's irritation thawed. He leaned over and whispered in her ear. "Can I ask you something?"

Chrissie widened her eyes. "Sure. What is it?"

With his hand atop hers, Dylan asked, "Would you be terribly upset if I killed Jayden?"

Although Chrissie didn't really approve of his crude joke, she found herself laughing at his foolishness. "Why would you want to kill Jay?"

"Well, I've been thinking about it." He scratched the fine hair along his temple. "I think the best way to settle our disagreement is to kill him. After all, no Jay, no problem."

Chrissie elbowed him in the side. "Stop talking nonsense before someone hears you, and calls security.

As he joked, Dylan's deep brown eyes danced with humor. "I'm serious. I've decided to wring his neck. You know, like they used to do chickens. I understand it's a painless procedure. Can't you just imagine him flopping around the ground with no head?"

Chrissie burst into laughter. "You're sick. You know that, don't you?"

"Your eyes are absolutely gorgeous when you laugh." He placed his hand over hers and squeezed. "Everything is going to be fine. We'll find your grandmother."

"I hope so, Dylan. I don't know what I'd do if anything happened to Nana. After my mother passed away, she raised me by herself. I don't understand why anyone would want to hurt her."

"We can't be certain of anything yet. Don't borrow trouble. There may be a logical explanation for all this."

Pretending to smile, she said, "We'll get to the bottom of this, won't we?"

"Of course, we will." He sat back and appeared to be deep in thought. Suddenly, he spoke. "Why did you choose Jayden? What's so special about him?"

To determine if anyone was listening, Chrissie turned and then peeked between the reclined seats. The man next to her dad appeared to be asleep. Even so, she didn't want to take any chances. "This isn't the place to talk about that."

"Okay. But will you tell me?"

"I'll tell you later."

"Do you promise?"

With a nod, she answered, "I promise." She bit her bottom lip. *"Not if I can find a way to wriggle out of it."*

* * * * *

When they arrived at Nana's residence, everything appeared normal. Chrissie expected to see the house laced with yellow tape, indicative of a crime scene. Either none had been placed there, or the strips had been removed. Standing in the shadows across the street, the threesome made their own assessment. Eyes sharp, William scanned every inch of the immediate area.

Unable to wait any longer, Chrissie broke ranks. She tried to dash for her former abode, but Dylan hooked her around the waist. With one arm, he spun her like an infant "What are you doing?" Her feet dangled in midair while she thrashed to free herself.

As usual, William took Dylan's side. "You can't go inside right now, Peanut. Suppose someone's in there." Once again, he scanned the perimeters of the building. "I can't detect anyone, but you never know."

"I've got to know, Daddy." Chrissie continued to wriggle. Tugging against the vice that restricted her, she demanded, "Let me go!" Her protests fell on deaf ears.

William stepped off the curb. "I'll go over." He gazed at his daughter. "You stay here with Dylan. If everything checks out, I'll call you." Like a phantom, he stole across the street, circled the house, then disappeared.

In a last ditch effort, Chrissie mustered all her strength. She shoved Dylan's stone chest, but the boa constrictor continued to squeeze. "Let me go."

Dylan rolled his eyes and grinned. "Nope." He exaggerated the sound of the 'p'. His enjoyment of Chrissie's predicament further annoyed her.

Thirty seconds later, William whispered

Chrissie's name from inside the house; Dylan placed her feet on the ground.

When her captor released his grip, Chrissie stomped his foot. "Jerk." Dylan beamed even wider. With her companion on her heels, she zipped across the street. The couple entered the house through a back window.

Statue-like, William stood in the living room. He raised his head and sniffed the air. "Scrutinize the house carefully, Peanut. Only you can determine any discrepancies."

With keen eyes, Chrissie studied her surroundings. Her graduation portrait no longer adorned the area above the hearth. *"My picture's missing,"* she mused, not sharing her thoughts. *"Maybe Nana decided to take it down."*

Careful to inspect every inch for clues, she prowled each room. In the living room, Dylan and William remained motionless, trying not to interfere with her inspection. She wandered into the bedroom, searching for anything to help locate her nana. Nothing seemed amiss until she examined the nightstand. The 8x10 picture of Chrissie that her grandmother kept on her night table had also been removed. Panicked, she rifled through her grandmother's cedar chest. Not only were all the pictures of Chrissie missing, but also all the mementos from her childhood. "Dad, everything is gone."

Deep grooves wrinkled William's brow as he

darted toward her. "What do you mean?" Before he reached her, Dylan held her in his arms.

The two men asked in sync, "What's missing, Chrissie?"

"There's not a picture of me in the house. The keepsakes Mama kept from my childhood are missing, as well."

Ever the intellectual, William regained his composure. "Let's examine this carefully before we jump to conclusions. What exactly is missing from your grandmother's room?"

Chrissie clamped Dylan's arm. "The locket with my hair in it, my teddy bear, my doll collection — everything."

"Could your grandmother have gotten rid of them after your..." William swallowed hard as though he found the word distasteful. "...death?"

"No. Absolutely not. Nana wouldn't have parted with anything that had to do with me. She had pictures of her great-grandmother that had faded with antiquity. Each time she opened a scrapbook she said, *'Nothing is more important than memories, and pictures keep people alive.'* If she said it once, she said it a thousand times."

Chrissie attempted to pull from Dylan's grasp, but he refused to let go. Together, they crept down the hall to her bedroom. Though she dreaded what lay beyond the entrance, she eased the door open. As she stepped into the room, a sense of doom gripped her frozen heart. "Everything looks the same." With a scowl, she shook her head. "Something is wrong." She shuffled to the bed and scrutinized it. "I know this sounds strange. Everything seems the same, but somehow it's all different." Dylan tilted his head in question and then alarm.

From the living room, William issued instructions. "Take your time, Christina. Think. What's different?" If his concern mirrored Chrissie's, he managed to maintain his poise.

Chrissie ran her hand across the bedspread, then sniffed the air. "This isn't my comforter. It looks like mine, but this one is different." Standing erect, she checked every aspect of the room. "Everything in this room is different. It doesn't even smell like me."

Head back, Dylan inhaled. "I can't be sure. I've only known your scent as a vampire." He drew in another breath. "You're right this room doesn't smell like you."

Terrified for her grandmother, Chrissie rushed to Dylan then buried her head in the crease of his arm. "Why would anyone break into the house, kidnap Nana, and take everything that belongs to me?"

Dylan massaged her back. "I don't know, but I *will* find out. I guarantee that." With narrowed eyes, he scanned the room, once more. "Let's get out of here."

When the pair reentered the living room, William was examining the back door. Dylan and Chrissie marched through the front room and into the kitchen. "Dad, have you found anything?"

William ran his hand along the molding of the door. "Yes. The garage door wasn't the only thing tampered with. This door has been removed from its hinges and replaced as well." He pointed near his feet. "Look at the floor closely. You can see tiny chips of paint. There are also small slivers of glass embedded in the fibers of the living room carpet."

Dylan eased away. He slipped into the living room to inspect the carpet.

William sniffed the air again. "I don't want to alarm you, but vampires have been here."

First, Chrissie gasped, then she covered her mouth. "What? Why? Since when does a vampire break into a house to attack someone?"

"Sweetheart, I said vampires. I detected more than one scent." As William continued to sniff, he scanned the room, searching every corner.. "The scent is faint, but multiple vampires have definitely been present in this house."

The sheer horror of his words sent Chrissie into convulsions.

Dylan bolted to her side. "Calm down, sweetheart." Wrapping his arms around her, he gazed into her eyes. "We're not sure she's been harmed."

In typical fashion, Chrissie wrenched her body from his hold. "Don't patronize me. You know as well as I do what happens to humans when vampires come into contact with them."

"Chrissie," William interrupted, "quiet down before someone hears you." He caressed her hand. "I haven't detected any blood. That means they took her with them."

"But why? Why take her? Nana's never hurt anybody."

"I don't know." Though William struggled to retain his poise, his shaky voice betrayed him. "Dylan, stay with Chrissie while I investigate the outside of the house."

Chrissie shook her head. "I'm going with you."

Stubborn as usual, Chrissie attempted to follow. However, Dylan grabbed her wrist. "Oh, no you're not."

Although Chrissie protruded her bottom lip, she didn't argue with him. "Alright," she said, as she tugged against his hand. "I couldn't defy both of you." She rolled her eyes at Dylan. "Besides. I don't feel like dangling in midair again."

Five minutes later, William returned. "Whoever did this, left an obvious trail. It's as though they wanted us to follow them."

Stepping toward her father, Chrissie asked, "What are we waiting for?"

Dylan tightened his grip on her wrist. "It sounds like a trap to me."

"He's right," William responded. "The signs are too obvious. No vampire would leave a trail like that without a motive."

Defeated, Chrissie slumped against Dylan. "Then what are we going to do?"

"The first thing we're going to do is to get a hotel room. When we have you settled, Dylan and I will follow the trail."

CHAPTER TEN
Clarifications

William rented an enormous suite. The elegant foyer served as the opening into a king's palace. At the entrance, two overstuffed chairs were situated atop a light blue marble floor. Their floral design perfectly complimented the border that encircled the top of the antique white wallpaper. Ficus trees stood on either side of the door, and provided the cozy touch hotel guests craved.

Chrissie ambled from room to room, scoping the layout. The bedrooms, two of them, were located on the right side of the foyer. Both contained ornate rustic chic furnishings. Rough against smooth textures created a comfortable, homey atmosphere. On the left of the foyer, a huge parlor, complete with both a living and dining area, had been decorated in neo-classic style.

While Dylan and her dad settled in the sitting room, Chrissie headed for the first bedroom, the smaller of the two. Once inside, she tossed her suitcase on the chair in the corner.

Dylan called from the living room. "Take the larger room."

When William leaned forward, Chrissie could

hear the squeak of the couch. "Yeah, Peanut, take the master bedroom. You may as well be comfortable."

Dylan rose from the sofa and marched down the hall. He leaned against the door to watch Chrissie turn on the television. "We'll only be here long enough to make our plans." He stepped through the entry. "Besides, don't women need more room for their little dainty things?" He wriggled his finger mockingly.

"I don't sleep, so why do I need a big bedroom?" Then, she answered her own question. "To sit in and worry."

He grabbed her luggage from the chair. "Lie across the bed and watch television, or read." Dylan led the way to the roomier chamber.

Chrissie had no desire to argue about trivial matters. She clicked off the set, and then trailed him. Upon entering the room, she noticed the bed first. A plush silky white comforter was adorned with matching accessories. The embellishments provided the perfect complement to the rustic furnishings. When Chrissie was a young girl, she would have been thoroughly impressed by the chic décor. However, with her grandmother's safety at issue, she held its beauty in contempt.

Once Dylan had her settled, he headed for the parlor. He and William needed to devise their plan.

Chrissie followed in hot pursuit. If nothing else,

she wanted to help formulate the details. She sat on the couch next to her father. "What should we do now?"

Focused on the floor, William spoke. "We're going back to the house to pick up the trail."

Chrissie bounced to her feet. "Great, I'll change and be ready to go in a flash."

William wrenched his head in her direction. "You're not going, Christina."

"I'm not staying behind." Chrissie tone sounded resolved, but she knew she couldn't win. In this instance, Dylan would surely back William. The two of them made an irresistible force. "You can't make me."

Dylan stated simply, "You're not going."

"Why can't I go?" In defense, Chrissie folded her arms.

As if trying to find the right words, Dylan turned to her. "Because when you walk, you're as loud as a buffalo thundering across the plains. I'm sorry, sweetheart. You would do more harm than good." Tact was never his forte.

With mouth agape, Chrissie slumped her shoulders. "Wow." She faced her dad for confirmation of Dylan's statement.

William stood, and then straightened his trousers. "He's right. We'd be so busy worrying about you, that we'd lose our concentration. That's how stupid mistakes are made."

Chrissie ambled across the room. She rested her posterior against the desk. "You don't need to worry about me. Physically, I'm almost as strong as you are."

Dylan sighed. "It has nothing to do with brute strength. You need training. I can hear you a mile away. You haven't even fully developed your sense of smell."

"But no human can hear me approaching."

In uncharacteristic fashion, William blared. "How many times do I have to tell you, you're not dealing with humans?" He seldom took a hard line with Chrissie. This, however, proved the exception. "Any vampire could effortlessly detect your presence." Shaking his head, he added, "If they couldn't see you, they'd hear you. If they couldn't hear you, they'd smell you."

She pounded her fist against the desk, causing the edge to splinter. "It isn't fair for the two of you to risk your lives for *my* grandmother. I should be doing something."

The corners of Dylan's mouth inched upward. "And so you shall. You'll be taking care of the one I love."

"He's right," William murmured, as he crossed the room to join her. "Besides, we don't know why they took items that belong to you. They may be trying to lure *you* into a trap."

Dylan narrowed the red margins of his lips, and raised his volume. "Nobody will ever touch you." Green highlights flashed through his brown irises. Chrissie realized how hollow her protests seemed in light of the severity of the situation. Though apprehensive, she resigned herself to stay behind.

While Dylan relaxed the muscles in his hands, he inhaled loudly. "Professor Garrett, I think I should take Chrissie to my home."

"You mean back to your apartment?"

"No. My village. She would be protected there. That way, we wouldn't need to worry about her while we were gone."

"Where is your village?"

"On Chogo Gangri in the Himalayas. My people burrowed into its side, forming passageways throughout. We've established our village in the interior of the mountain."

"Inside a mountain." The skepticism in William's tone resonated. He furrowed his brow. "How long has this village been there?"

"For hundreds of years. No one has ever discovered it — and lived."

"So it has been discovered before."

"Yes. But as I said, no one has ever reported their findings."

William ignored that fact as his curiosity had been piqued. "What's the elevation?"

"Approximately 28,000 feet."

His thirst for knowledge endless, William continued to press. "The climate?"

"It's cold, of course, but the mountain protects us from the elements. Over the centuries, our bodies have become acclimated to the weather. It's our natural environment now."

William placed his hands behind his back. With one clasping the other, he paced the floor. "Are you telling me that six thousand people live inside one mountain?"

"Not all of us reside within the mountain. Like me, some have established homes in the human world."

Finally, William focused on the reason for the discussion. "How would we get her there?"

Dylan smiled. "We would take a plane part of the way, and I would carry her part of the way myself. It would, however, take a few days to make the trip."

Seemingly perplexed, William ogled Dylan. "You would carry her part of the way. Why would you carry her?"

"There are things you don't know about me." Dylan turned his back to them. His voice barely a whisper, he admitted. "It's time for you to learn who I really am."

Chrissie gasped. "What do you mean?" She found it difficult to believe there were things about him she didn't know.

"We'll go for a drive, find a secluded spot, and then I'll show you."

* * * * *

Dylan rented a car and drove to a spot on the lake that was closed for the season. After the threesome exited the car, Chrissie and Dylan held hands as they strolled into the brush. When the company reached a clearing, Dylan released her hand. He stepped three paces ahead. "Stand back. I need room." As though he were pushing her back without actually touching her, he extended his arm, the palm of his hand facing her.

Chrissie eased back several steps. Fear of what she would discover gripped her soul. As she gawked, William grabbed her arm and yanked her away.

Dylan removed his shirt. He turned his back to his companions, exposing what resembled two long scars. The marks ran the length of his shoulder blades. After that, he removed his shoes. Folding his arms against his chest, he bent his midsection. Next, he flexed his rhomboid muscles. The expanse of his bare back astounded Chrissie. His muscles rippled, and the scars suddenly exploded, releasing two enormous wings. Their entire span measured at least twelve feet. When he straightened, he faced them. Emerald eyes glowed in the darkness. Chrissie parted her lips as she observed claw-like hands and feet. His hairline had shifted into a point that joined at his brow, and he appeared two inches taller. Apart from that, his facial features remained unchanged. When Chrissie saw his imposing figure, she took an involuntary breath.

With outstretched arms, he glanced at Chrissie. "What you see before you is the true nature of a drachmon, Christina." His voice reverberated when he spoke.

The sight of his green eyes ablaze in the moonlight both frightened and thrilled her. Astonishment, horror, and utter adoration flooded her simultaneously. She shoved William's hand away, and then sprinted into Dylan's arms. "I love you, Dylan," she murmured and showered him with kisses.

He swept her off her feet. Like a babe in arms, he cradled her close to him. Fluttering his expansive wings, he soared straight up. As Dylan circled, Chrissie shouted to her father. "Don't wait for us. We'll meet you back at the hotel."

Their flight allowed Chrissie to view the world from Dylan's vantage point. For thirty minutes, they flew nonstop. When they descended into the Santa Cruz Mountains, she found herself mesmerized by the magnificence of the scenery from the sky. The redwoods, enveloped by a purple haze, climbed toward the heavens. Likewise, a yellow and pinkish mist had settled over the horizon. The sight proved utterly breathtaking.

The couple landed among the trees. With care, Dylan set Chrissie on her feet. A huge grin lit his features. "So, how'd you enjoy your first flight?"

"It was awesome."

"I'm glad you enjoyed it," he said, as he pulled away, "but we really need to talk."

Not wanting the exhilaration she felt to end, Chrissie flattened her lips. "Are you going to get all serious on me now?" She turned and walked several paces away. With her back to him, she asked, "Can't we just enjoy the moment?"

Dylan strolled to her, closing the gap she had created. "I wish we had that luxury." His voice reverberated as he wrapped her in his arms. "In a few hours we'll need to start our journey to Carthexia."

She flinched at the echo in his tone. *"Wow. I've never heard anything like that before."* Curious, she faced him. "What's Carthexia?"

"It's my village." He pulled her near. "Before we go, there are some things you need to know."

"Like what?"

He sat on the grass, then pulled her into his lap. "When we get there, I'm going to tell everyone that you've agreed to be my exclusive consort."

"Why?"

"Because, the male populace outnumbers the female population by ten to one. If the warriors believe I've claimed you, they won't dare touch you. You see, the penalty for the seduction of a nobleman's consort is death by decapitation. But if you're not promised, you'd be considered fair game. That means any alpha male could take you if he so desires."

Eyes wide, Chrissie spoke softly, "Anyone?" She swallowed hard.

"We honor our females," he explained, his breath warm on her cheek, "but you'd be considered an outworlder. Unless you have the protection of being a warrior's exclusive consort, you wouldn't be subject to the same treatment as our females."

Chrissie plucked a blade of grass from the ground. "Okay." Then, it occurred to her what he had said. "You're a nobleman?"

"Yes. My mother is queen." He sounded as though his comments were the most natural things in the world.

With one brow raised, she mocked. "Oh. So you're a prince." Chrissie didn't fully believe him. However, if it were true, it cleared up the question of his arrogance.

At first Dylan grinned, but then he furrowed his brow. "Remember. Don't tell anyone you're not pledged to be my consort, not even a female. No one can know." Holding her face in his hands, he scrutinized her countenance. "Do you understand?"

She nodded. "I understand, but I can take care of myself."

"Christina, we're not talking about human males. Against a human, you're virtually indestructible. Against a drachmon, you would find yourself as vulnerable as any human female. You wouldn't stand a chance. That's why you're going to start your training while you are there."

"Training?" Chrissie repeated, as she hugged his neck.

"Yes. Before you come back here, you need to know how to fight."

"Hum." She placed the blade of grass between her lips. "I like that idea." The notion of training for combat thrilled her, not to mention the thought of being Dylan's mate.

Impishly, he smirked. "I thought you would." He removed the blade of grass from her mouth and kissed her tenderly. "Chrissie."

She snuggled against his neck. "Huh?"

Dylan rested his head atop hers. "Tell me the truth about your relationship with Jayden."

Annoyed, Chrissie pulled away. Her focus on the ground, she complained. "Everything was going so well. Why do we have to spoil it by talking about Jay again?"

"Look at me, baby."

Turning her head, she averted her gaze. "No. I don't want to."

"Baby." His voice was utterly melodic. The urge to smile swept over Chrissie; she tightened her lips. He kissed her cheek. "My love."

She tucked her bottom lip beneath her front teeth, but her upturned lips revealed her mirth. Her resolve melted by his charm, she acquiesced. "What do you want to know?"

"Why did you choose him?"

An uncomfortable notion filled Chrissie's thoughts. *"I'm going to regret this."* She inhaled, then blew the air out through expanded cheeks. "I've known Jay since I was ten years old. He's always been there for me. My father knew I would need a loyal familiar." She shrugged. "So, he brought him to me."

"I thought you said you didn't know your father until after your transformation."

"That's true. Although I didn't know it at the time, he'd been watching over me for years. I guess he noticed Jay hanging around all the time."

With a scowl, Dylan asked, "He's been hanging around you since you were ten?"

"Humph, he shouldn't have asked." Chrissie stood and slowly walked away. "I told you I've known him all my life."

Dylan rose. "So, how does it work?"

Leaning against a redwood, she watched as he made his way toward her. "What do you mean?"

Hands on either side of her, he placed his palms against the tree. "I mean, your father chose Jayden. Why exactly did he choose him?"

"Well." She closed one eye and flinched in anticipation of his reaction. "See, a familiar can't be just anyone. He has to be someone who has an interest in your welfare before the initiation."

"Explain." The reverberation in his voice echoed like sound waves striking the wall of a cave.

Chrissie allowed her head to rest on the tree, her eyes elevated. "A familiar shares more than his blood with a vampire. He knows your secrets. When you're vulnerable, he protects you." She lowered her gaze to meet his. "He would die for you, so he has to be someone you trust without reservation."

"Is that why that drone wouldn't back down?"

She bit her lip and wriggled her nose. "Ugh, yeah."

Dylan lowered his arms. This time, he walked away. "Did your father realize how much he loves you?"

"I don't know." Chrissie followed in his footsteps. "Since I'm being honest, I may as well tell you everything." Wrapping her arms around him, she squeezed gently. *"I'm going to regret this."* While she searched for the right words, she paused. "Er. Well see. When Dad first brought Jay to me, I told him the truth about what I am, and what he'd be getting into. I thought it would only be fair to let him decide. I would've released him if he hadn't chosen to remain with me. He chose to be my familiar, so..." Through clenched teeth, she blurted the last part. "When I initiated him, I fused my blood with his."

He turned to face her. "What are you telling me, Christina?"

"I hate it when he calls me Christina." She chose her words carefully. "Although he's still alive, and he still has blood in his veins, he's actually more vampire than human."

A rumble erupted deep in Dylan's chest. However, he asked very calmly, "In what ways is he more a vampire?"

His calm demeanor made Chrissie more nervous than his anger. "He's extremely strong. Although he *is* aging, you'd never know it." She scratched her head.

Dylan tightened his jaws; the veins protruded on either side. "Is that all?"

She sat on the grass. "Not really."

Fists knotted, he continued to press. "What else?"

Chrissie reached for his hand and tugged him down beside her. "Umm, if I want to, I can contact him mentally."

Although he sat next to her, Dylan's muscles remained taut. "Are you saying you can communicate with him telepathically?"

She squeezed her eyes shut, pressed her lips together, then opened one eye. "Yes. And he can communicate with me."

Like a tightly wound spring, Dylan bounced up. "Then, why didn't he contact you about your grandmother?"

Again, Chrissie reached for his hand. In a soothing manner, she explained, "I have to initiate the connection. If I don't summon him, he can't contact me."

Dylan sat back down and growled, "Is that everything?"

She sighed, and confessed. "If I do make the connection, and he's anywhere within a ten miles radius of me, he can find me, and vice versa. It's like radar."

"What else?" he snarled.

"I can also see through his eyes." Chrissie scratched her ear. "If I let him, he can see through mine."

He pointed a finger at her. "So you're saying you're literally in his blood — he's a part of you."

Chrissie winced. "That would be correct." Dylan nodded his head then rolled his eyes. After a few seconds, he shook his head. While she watched, Chrissie mused. *"I wonder if he's confused."*

"Only *you*, Christina, would do something that ridiculous."

She sprang up. "Are you calling me stupid?" It wasn't *what* he said. It was *how* he said it.

Red-faced, Dylan leaped to his feet. "I didn't call you stupid. I said what you did was ridiculous."

Hands on her hips, Chrissie shot back. "I don't see what's so ridiculous about it. Jay's always been a loyal friend. He deserves to be more than merely someone I call when I need something."

"He is *not* your friend. He's your familiar."

"I beg to differ. He's been my friend since I was ten years old. He chose an existence like mine in order to help me. I call that friendship."

Emerald specks sparked in Dylan's eyes, the usual signal of his ire. "And I call that *love*."

Frustrated, Chrissie threw her hands in the air. "Why do you persist in dwelling on this?"

"Because I saw how that drone looks at you." Dylan gesticulated, extending his arms like a preacher in a pulpit. "That man is totally and completely bewitched. Now, I know why. You're literally in his blood."

Lips tight, she muttered, "Let's talk about something else. I really don't want to argue tonight."

With wings extended, he stormed away. "We should get back. We have a lot to do."

Chrissie grew concerned. With his back to her, she leaned her head against his arm. "Why are you angry with me?" She intentionally sounded like the injured party.

Laying his head against hers, he replied, "I'm not really angry, Chrissie. That's just who you are."

To avoid another argument, Chrissie didn't ask what he meant. Instead, she put her arms around him and tiptoed to kiss his neck. "I'm sorry I got angry."

Dylan turned then pulled her to him. "I'm sorry too. Maybe Jayden is a subject we need to avoid."

"That sounds good."

"However, broken necks are fashionable this year."

Before she opened her mouth, he kissed her. When Dylan took her in his arms, Chrissie forgot about Jayden and their disagreement. Butterflies fluttered their way down her abdomen, and she panted. "Dylan."

His breathing labored, he murmured, "Yes," and lifted her off her feet until their faces met.

Chrissie wrapped her arms around his neck, and her legs around his hips. Kissing him softly, she whispered, "We could be telling the truth when we say I'm your consort."

"What are you saying?" He searched her face.

"I want you. I want you, now." Her words stunned her. Nonetheless, they were true. She ached for him.

Dylan set her down. With no hesitation, he replied, "No."

Stunned, Chrissie shoved him away. "What?" More hurt than angry, she stumbled back. "You don't want me?"

"Baby. I want you more than I've ever wanted a female in my life. I've tried every trick to get next to you, but I don't want you like this."

All Chrissie heard was, "*I don't want you,*" and his words devastated her. She spun to storm away, but Dylan clutched her arm. Although she struggled to free herself, he maintained his iron grip. "Let me go."

"You don't understand what I'm saying. I want you so bad it hurts." He pulled her into his arms. "I want you the right way—when you're ready, not because you're afraid of what might happen."

She balked at his assumption. "Is that what you think? I want you because I'm afraid."

Dylan took a deep breath and sighed. "You've resisted me time and time again. Why would you give in tonight?"

Unable to meet his gaze, she stared at the ground. Her lips trembled as she admitted the truth. "Because, I love you, and I need you."

"I love you too." Dylan kissed her tenderly. Resting his head atop hers, he explained, "When we make love, I don't want you to have any regrets." He kissed the top of her hair. "We'll both know when the time is right."

CHAPTER ELEVEN
The Body

Dylan flew back to the city. He landed outside of town in an area protected by the cover of trees. When the couple strolled into their hotel suite, William stood motionless, a frown etched upon his pasty face.

Her dad had mimicked human mannerism so long, that it was second nature to him. For him to stand that still, Chrissie knew something serious had happened. "What's wrong, Dad?"

William moved his head mechanically as he looked at her. "I was just about to write you a note, when I heard you coming."

Anxious, Dylan advanced. "What's the matter?"

William walked across the room. He placed his hand on her back. "Let's sit down, Christina."

Anger and fear, engulfed her. She jerked away. "I don't want to sit down, Daddy. What's wrong?"

Reaching for her hand, William held it between his. "The police called." His voice broke. "They've found the body of a female that matches your grandmother's description. They need someone to make the identification." He glanced at Dylan. "I was headed out when you arrived."

Chrissie closed her eyes. When she opened them, the hysteria she felt showed through with crystal clarity. "I'm coming with you."

"You can't come with me." William released her hand. "You grew up in this town. Suppose someone recognizes you."

Dylan placed his arm protectively around her lower back. "I don't like this. There had been no progress in the case for a month." Chrissie buried her head in the crease of his arm, and he enfolded her. The warmth of his body soothed her. "Suddenly we arrive, and they find a body. It smells like a trap to me."

"I agree," William walked to the coffee table to retrieve his keys, "but what can we do? We need to ascertain exactly what information they've gathered." He sauntered across the room to join the couple.

Dylan, who hadn't taken his eyes off Chrissie, placed his hand on her father's shoulder. "Well, you're not going alone. I'll go with you."

As he reclaimed his jacket from the chair, William issued his instructions. "Chrissie." She turned to face her father. "You stay here. We can't take the chance of having someone recognize you. Jayden will arrive soon. He can keep you company."

Chrissie glanced at Dylan. "When did you hear from Jay?" She cringed, waiting for the hammer to drop.

"You left your cell phone here. After I heard from the police, he called. I told him what happened, and you know him. He said he would be on the next flight."

In her heart, Chrissie rejoiced that Jayden would be with her. "You should have told him *not* to come."

"Humph, stop Jayden from coming when he thinks you may need him," William laughed nervously, "are you kidding?"

"I see what you mean." She mimicked a smile.

Dylan rolled his eyes. "Why did you give that drone your cell number?"

"Stop it, Dylan. We don't have time for that." Chrissie retorted, her nerves already frayed.

Though he continued to ogle her, Dylan made no further comment about Jayden. "I still think something is wrong."

Coat in hand, William headed for the door with Dylan in his tracks. "We'll know more when we get there."

CHAPTER TWELVE
Crisis

While Chrissie waited for her men to return, she decided to watch television to occupy her mind. *Burden*, one of her favorite TV shows, was airing an episode she'd already seen. Not one to indulge in past pleasures, she flipped through the channels. Since nothing captured her attention, she flung the remote on the sofa.

Bored, Chrissie headed to the bedroom. When she entered the chamber, she grabbed her backpack from the bed. At the airport, she had purchased a new novel, so she dug in her knapsack to retrieve it.

Chrissie stretched out on the bed to read, while reflections of her grandmother filled her head. Unable to concentrate, she decided to daydream about Dylan. Contrary to her desire, sometimes the mind does what it wants to do. She found herself enthralled by images of her youth. In particular, she remembered the wonderful times spent chatting with her nana in the kitchen. She shook her head to dislodge the thoughts. Even pleasant memories of her grandmother proved unwelcomed at that moment.

Frustrated, Chrissie drifted back into the parlor

to find something interesting to watch. Her request was answered when the door to the suite crashed off its hinges, and then splintered into bits. Startled, she leaped to her feet. Two enormous brutes, which she quickly recognized as vampires, bolted through the threshold. As if cloned, their resemblance astonished her. Both stood over six feet, one taller by a fraction of an inch. They wore matching outfits, khakis, and green shirts. Each looked to be about twenty, with closely cropped, spiked red hair.

Snarling, Chrissie flipped over the couch to create a barricade between her and the assailants. She landed in a crouching position, poised and ready to strike. With her barrier in place, she evaluated her predicament to devise an effective strategy of defense.

Before Chrissie could formulate a plan, her attackers advanced. From both sides, they flanked her. She'd never had to defend herself, so she had no idea how to counter their attack. Hoping for the advantage of speed, Chrissie leaped over the couch and sprinted for the door. Just as her foot touched the doorstep, the taller of the two grabbed her leg, and dragged her back inside. Marshaling all her strength, she kicked fruitlessly against his hand. He clenched her legs together in a vise. The other lifted Chrissie from the floor, seized both her arms, and penned them behind her back.

As Chrissie thrashed, the pair hauled her toward the window. With Herculean effort, she managed to wrench one leg free. She smashed the heel of her shoe into the larger male's jaw. Although the blow caused his head to jerk backward, she'd inflicted only minimal damage. Frantic, she struggled to strike another blow. However, he caught her foot and clamped it next to the other. When they reached the window, he released her legs and jumped out. Still battling, Chrissie stomped the smaller male's foot. The blow had no more effect than a mouse scurrying across his appendage. He tightened his grip, boxing her arms against her sides.

As Chrissie flailed, the smaller assailant lifted her off her feet and attempted to toss her out the window. Elevated, she was able to brace her feet against the window's frame. With her limbs planted, she used her head and shoulders for leverage. She strained against the goon with all the power she possessed. Like lightning, he flipped her, hurling her head first, out the window. During her descent, she tucked her knees close to her torso. Then, she twisted her body and twirled so she'd land on her feet.

Positioned beneath the window, the larger brute caught Chrissie by the legs. This maneuver left her arms free; she dug her granite nails into his face. He howled in agony, stumbled back and released his hold. Taking advantage of his injury, Chrissie released her fangs. She sank them into his neck as hard and deep as possible. The sound of his tearing flesh thrilled her. When she jerked her daggers away, a large section of his jugular had been severed. She spat the rancid flesh into his anguished face. Mutilated, he writhed in agony. Very little can cause a vampire pain, but Chrissie knew the bite of another vampire was excruciating. As she prepared for a second attack, the smaller guy joined the melee. He wrapped his massive arms around her and yanked her away. In an effort to loosen his grip, Chrissie drove the bottom of her foot into his knees. The larger hulk, however, had recovered enough to seize her legs. Though Chrissie continued to struggle, her efforts proved useless. While they towed her to their waiting car, she heard someone shouting her name from above. "Christina," Jayden yelled.

When Chrissie looked up, she saw Jayden launch himself from the third floor window. He landed with a thud. Afraid he had hurt himself, she screamed in terror. Contrary to her fears, he bounced to his feet. With fury in his footsteps, he dashed toward the captors.

Focused on Jayden, the lengthier culprit dropped her legs, and advanced toward him. Like two tigers, the adversaries stalked each other. "Take the girl and go," he hissed over his shoulder. "I've got this." Chrissie hoped she had inflicted enough damage to give Jay an edge.

Immediately, Jayden hurled himself at the stone-like body. The hulk stepped aside with such alacrity that when Jay reached him, he already stood sideways. As Jayden passed him, the brute caught him in a chokehold.

Panicked, Chrissie braced her body against her

attacker. "Let me go," she screamed. Her one thought consisted of helping Jayden.

Continuing to wriggle, Chrissie drew her legs up as high as she could manage, then drove them into the goon's knees. At last, she managed to loosen his grip enough to sink her fangs into his forearm. Unlike the taller bruiser, he barely seemed to notice. *"This guy must have been made of cast iron. Nothing but a machine could have withstood the force of that bite without reacting. I injected enough venom to bring down an elephant."*

Once Chrissie clamped down on her enemy's flesh again, she saw Jay swing his leg behind his aggressor for leverage. He spun, and then threw his weight into the culprit. Using his fist as a hammer, he drove the perpetrator to the ground. His adversary rebounded at hypersonic speed. In a flash, he leaped to his feet, crouched, and lunged at Jayden. Wrapping his powerful hands around Jay's neck, he executed a strangle hold. Although Jayden stumbled under the force of the attack, he easily regained his momentum. Jay reached over the barbarian's arms and used two fingers to jab him in the trachea. Stunned, the lout gasped for air and released his grip on Jay's neck. Faster than Chrissie thought him capable, he punched the thug in the windpipe then followed with a kick to his chest, knocking him to the ground.

Jayden's antagonist bound to his feet and flew at him with the speed of a cougar. Once he caught Jay, he grabbed both his wrists from behind.

Although unprepared for the assault, Jay reacted with expertise. Stepping out, he turned, rotated his wrists, and freed them. Faster than the blink of an eye, he seized the clod's wrist and yanked his arm straight out, exposing his torso. Into the air he sprang, and then crashed down on the cad's vulnerable ribs. The force of the impact sent his opponent spiraling to the ground. With the strength of five men, Jayden smashed his fist into the lummox's ear. Flesh and bone collided in a brutal aftermath.

After that, Chrissie didn't want to see anymore. She never released her hold on the hooligan's arm. Yet, he continued to drag her to the car. Jayden had his hands full with his foe, which forced Chrissie to fend for herself. Once Chrissie's captor hauled her to the vehicle, his patience was spent. He drew back his fist, and with no thought to her gender, drove the side of her face into the doorframe. The force of the impact crumpled the exterior.

Although fleeting, agonizing pain surged through the side of Chrissie's head. She hadn't experienced any type of physical discomfort in more than seven years. This blow stunned her more mentally than physically. As darkness wafted over her, she heard a blood-curdling shriek reverberate in the distance. The ruffian shoved her into the car, sprinted to the driver's seat, and sped away. Before she slipped into oblivion, she smiled. "You know, he's going to kill you, right?"

* * * * *

Unaware of how much time had elapsed, Chrissie drifted in and out of consciousness. Her responsiveness returned when the speeding car suddenly lurched. Like a knife, a grating scraped against the metal, and screeched across the dome. Simultaneously, a sharp claw pierced the top of the car; then, another. After two more penetrations, a rectangular pattern was formed through the roof. The car was pitched from side to side as a succession of powerful blows pulverized the roof.

Though the assault only lasted seconds, it seemed an eternity to Chrissie. Amazed, she watched, while Dylan slammed his fist into the car. His wild eyes glowed as he sliced one claw through the back of the goon's neck. The antagonist howled in pain and flailed aimless. He tried in vain to break Dylan's grip. However, Dylan growled viciously and dug his other claw deeply into his shoulder.

Holding the car with his back claws, Dylan barked orders at Chrissie. "Take the wheel, and head back to town. I'll be back in a minute."

Chrissie looked into the face of love. Although Dylan's features were distorted by the rage which consumed him, he was still beyond handsome. She reached for the wheel, but her assailant seized her wrist. Instinctively, she screamed. The green in Dylan's eyes flashed, and he roared. The volume shook the very foundation of the car. He snatched his iron claw from the villain's neck. To gain momentum, he drew his arm back and thrust his claw through the fiend rotator cuff, severing his arm. The appendage still gripped Chrissie's wrist when it fell to the seat. She tossed it in the backseat, and then grabbed the wheel.

With supersonic speed, Dylan thrust his claw back into the guy's neck. He beat his wings, creating tension between the gorilla's collarbone and his body. Releasing his back claws, he soared straight up. The bushwhacker's neck made a ripping sound as Dylan tore his head from his shoulder. With one hand, he hurled the head so far, even Chrissie didn't see where it landed.

Reaching into the car, he yanked the rest of the body out. Blood splattered onto the seat, as well as Chrissie's blouse. "Go back to the hotel, Chrissie," he ordered, before flying away. Chrissie gladly obeyed his command. Never before had any growl sounded so wonderful.

CHAPTER THIRTEEN
The Aftermath

It took five minutes to return to the hotel. Apparently, Chrissie had only been unconscious for a brief time. Not wanting anyone to see the damage to the automobile, she parked three blocks away, then sprinted the short distance. When she arrived, the police were already outside and investigating the scene. William and Jayden had cleared away all evidence of her attackers.

Aware of how suspicious it would look for her to make an unexpected appearance after her abduction, Chrissie hid in the shadows to observe the outcome of her ordeal. William darted his eyes in her direction, acknowledging her presence.

A middle-aged gentleman with a receding hairline led the investigation. A gentle breeze ruffled the thin wisps of hair that encircled his head. The fabric on the elbows of his suit appeared frayed from many years of wear. He had all the signs of an underpaid public servant. The officer charged her dad. Pulling a small black notebook from his pocket, he began the inquisition. "Does your daughter have any enemies?"

William folded his arms. "No," he answered,

"none."

"Do you know of anyone who would have any reason to take her?"

Her father shifted his weight from one foot to the other. "No. No one had anything against my daughter. We've only been in town for a few hours."

The detective scribbled the answers in his pad. "Why are you here?"

"We're here on vacation."

"The desk clerk says another young man arrived with you. Where is he?" The investigator's complacent expression didn't conceal the suspicion in his tone.

From the hard lines in her dad's face, Chrissie could tell he was getting annoyed. "He's searching for my daughter."

The sergeant turned his back, and then walked several paces. "Why would he be searching for your daughter?" He faced William. "Is he familiar with our city?"

Before he answered, Chrissie saw William bite the inside of his jaw. "No. He isn't. I told you we've only been in this city for a few hours. He's just trying to help."

"Great! That's all we need—inexperienced strangers prowling our streets in search of a missing girl." He pointed his chin at Jayden, who was being checked out by an emergency medic. "Who is he?" From Jay's tattered appearance, he'd clearly been involved in a violent brawl.

"He's a family friend."

As the medic bandaged Jayden's arm, the detective inspected him from head to toe. "How did he just happen to be here when all this took place?"

William shoved his hands into his pocket. "Fortunately, he arrived while I was out."

"*Fortunately*," the sergeant repeated sarcastically. "Humph, so what is his relationship with your daughter?"

Tight-lipped, William then replied, "They're friends. I told you that."

"Um ugh, what is her relationship with the young man who is searching for her?"

Though it had taken a while, William's irritation with the asininity of the conversation surfaced. The volume of his voice rose two octaves. "He's her boyfriend."

Undeterred, the detective spewed more accusations. "Is she dating both of them?" The man seemed bent on creating the worst possible scenario.

"No." William's tone resembled a growl.

"*Really.* Let me see if I understand this." The

officer pulled a cigar from his pocket. "It's evident an altercation took place here. Your daughter is missing. Her boyfriend is missing, and *he*," the detective scoffed, indicating Jayden, "looks like he's been hit by a Mac truck. If you were me, what would you think?" He struck a match, cupped his hands, and lit his cigar. Once he extinguished the flame, he tossed it on the ground.

William made a fist. "I think I'd investigate the evidence, not make snide innuendoes."

"Right," the detective remarked offhandedly while he sauntered over to interrogate Jayden. "So, what's your relationship with the young lady?"

Sitting in the back of the ambulance, Jay glanced up. "Her name is Christina."

The sergeant sneered. "Okay. What's your relationship with Christina?" He blew cigar smoke in Jay's face.

Jayden tilted his head in the opposite direction. "Why? What does that have to do with anything?"

Hidden by the shadow of an oak tree, Chrissie jumped when Dylan touched her shoulder. She had been listening so intently that she hadn't heard him approach.

In one movement, Dylan whirled her around and then wrapped her in his arms. "Are you alright?"

Beaming with gratitude, Chrissie caressed his

face. "I'm fine, now that I'm with you."

Dylan swept disheveled hair from her face. "Did he hurt you?" He still trembled with rage.

"No." Her voice was softer than usual.

He inspected her face for signs of injury. "When I saw him hit you..." His words trailed off, and he frowned at the memory.

Though Chrissie had an odd sensation in her head, she lied, "I told you; I'm fine." The blow to her head must have caused considerable damage. Since her transformation, she had not experienced such pain. She squinted, then closed one eye tightly. "Are you okay?"

Tightening his fists against her back, he held her close. "No. When I think of how close he came to taking you away, I get furious. I should've known better than to leave you alone. Too many things didn't add up." Chrissie could hear his heart thundering in his chest.

"No one took me away from you. I'm here." She placed her palm on his cheek. "I'm not going anywhere."

Dylan stroked her hand, held it next to his face, then kissed her palm. "The thought of losing you is more than I can bear." When he touched her, his heart rate slowed and his muscles relaxed. Abruptly, he shifted his attention to the hotel. "What happened while I was gone?"

"They think it was a brawl. I guess they feel you and Jay fought over me."

He puckered his lips and nodded his head. "Not a bad idea. Wonder what the lizard would taste like?"

Chrissie punched his arm. "Behave." She chuckled. "What are we going to do? I can't just show up."

"Well. We could say I caught up with your assailant and ran him off the road. We fought, and he ran away. They can't prove anything. They'll take your statement, have you look at some mug shots, and then let you go."

Chrissie shook her head. "That doesn't sound plausible to me. Wouldn't it be better for them to find me roaming around with a concussion? That way I wouldn't remember anything, so I couldn't provide any information."

"Nope. They'd have to take you to the hospital to have you checked out." He placed his hand on her heart. "You can't do that." He clenched his fists. "Besides. As long as there's someone out there trying to take you, I'm not leaving you alone."

Chrissie backed away. "Do you really think they were after me?"

"Don't you? What are the chances of someone kidnapping your grandmother, and then two vampires trying to kidnap you? No. Somebody wants you. I don't know who, and I don't know why, but I *will* find out."

"But there's no reason anyone would want me. What would they have to gain?"

"I don't know." He stroked his temple. That's what we have to find out."

Finally noticing Dylan's bare chest, Chrissie stroked his pectoral muscle. "Where's your shirt?"

Dylan glanced down, then touched his pecs. "Oh, it's in your father's car."

Chrissie chuckled. "Are you purposefully trying to tempt me?"

He laughed. "Yeah, right." He kissed her brow. "You have a will of iron."

CHAPTER FOURTEEN

Business As Usual

Driving home from the airport proved somewhat thorny. To avoid further conflict, Chrissie sat in the front seat with her dad. The animosity between Dylan and Jayden festered like a sore. William made several lame jokes to lighten the mood, but neither of them responded. Soon, even William's demeanor soured.

Chrissie listened to all the bickering she could stand. Between Jayden's growls and Dylan's snarls, she'd finally had enough. Leaning over the seat, she chastised her quarreling companions. "With the way the two of you are acting, it's a wonder the cops didn't throw both of you in jail."

Dylan placed his arm on the front seat. "What are you talking about? We're being civil to each other." He rolled his eyes at Jayden. "There's no blood on the fool. I haven't cracked his worthless skull, *yet*."

Jayden wrenched his head in Dylan's direction. "Any time you're feeling froggy, freak, jump."

Dylan snickered. "Humph. Is that a sample of your *drone-like* wit?"

"I don't know what you mean by drone-like, but if you say another word, I'll *drone* my fist into your…"

William clamped down on the steering wheel." Enough!" His volume shook the car. "Someone tried, and almost succeeded in kidnapping my daughter tonight." Taking his eyes off the road, he glared at the pestilent pair. "All you two can think about is your pride. We have a serious crisis here. We don't have time for foolishness." He faced the highway. "If you can't conduct yourselves with some decorum, I'll ask both of you to leave."

Both men answered simultaneously. "Sorry, sir."

"Alright then, let's talk about what transpired tonight. Chrissie, tell us exactly what happened."

Explaining how she battled her attackers, Chrissie swelled with pride. She recounted everything that happened from the time the two thugs burst through the door until she bit them.

Once she had finished her narration, Jayden began his tale. "Well. As you know, I called Chrissie, and you answered, Professor Garrett. That's when you told me about the body the police had found. I decided to catch the next flight out…"

Dylan cut his eyes at Jayden. "Tell us something we don't know, skunk."

Chrissie was about to chastise Dylan when William spoke up. "Dylan, I wasn't joking about sending you away if you can't conduct yourself properly." Dads were very handy sometimes.

"Yes sir. Sorry." Chrissie had never seen him so compliant. She glanced over her shoulder and grinned. Unsure of whether his acquiescence steamed from his concern, or his respect for her father, she liked it.

William careened his head to the side. "Continue, Jay."

"As I was saying before I was so rudely interrupted. When I arrived at the hotel, I asked the desk clerk for your room number. He gave it to me, and I went up. Once I got to the third floor, I saw the door to your room had been knocked off the hinges, so I rushed inside. One of the plants in the foyer had been overturned. I searched the suite, looking for Chrissie. As I entered the bedroom, I saw this huge figure bounding out the window. When I ran over, I saw Chrissie being dragged away by two hulking thugs. That's when I jumped out the window."

Dylan slammed his fist against the door, concaving it. The car lurched and Chrissie winced. Everyone gawked at him, but remained silent. Chrissie looked at her father. Although externally, William retained his composure, she knew inside he seethed with rage as well.

With Dylan's episode at an end, Jay cleared his throat. "I heard this guy yell, '*Take the girl and go.*' I don't know why, but I didn't realize they were vampires until I saw the first one move. I handled him pretty easily though. Chrissie had already taken a plug out of him."

Dylan grinned, then winked at her. "That's my baby," he crowed. Jayden glared at him.

Shifting his weight to one side, William glanced over his shoulder. "He said take the girl and go? Are you sure that's what he said?"

"Yeah. I heard him clearly. Anyway," Jayden continued, "while I was fighting this guy, I saw the other one dragging Chrissie to a car. I don't know what I would have done if you two hadn't shown up when you did."

Chrissie scanned the faces of the three men. "What happened to that goon Jay fought?"

Leaning forward, Dylan responded, "We took care of him."

"What did you do to him?"

Without taking his eyes off the road, William explained, "We dismembered him. After that, we put his body in the incinerator."

Still concerned, Chrissie looked to her father for comfort. "Since you destroyed both of them, does that mean it's over?"

"No, baby, someone sent them. They didn't know you. They had no reason to attack you, unless someone else was behind this."

Dylan rubbed her shoulder. "One of them said, 'Take the girl and go.' That means they came specifically for you."

"Why me? I've never done anything to anybody."

William glanced at his daughter. "I need you to understand something. The world is filled with deadly creatures, some as lethal as vampires." Dylan lifted his powerful hand from her shoulder; she understood what her dad meant. "Someone is determined to get you, so you'll need to be extremely careful. That means you can't go back to school."

"What?" She frowned. "What do you want me to do, hide in the house?"

Dylan leaned forward, his tone harsh. "If that's what it takes." Chrissie understood he wasn't angry with her. His frustration made him irritable.

Jayden rose in his seat and bristled. "Don't yell at her!"

"Look," Chrissie interrupted before they had a chance to start another argument. "I'm not staying home. If someone wants me badly enough, he will find a way to get me no matter where I am."

In an attempt to calm the rising animosity, William spoke in a soothing tone. "We'll talk about this later."

Her arms folded, Chrissie sat back in her seat.

"There's nothing to talk about. By the way, what happened at the police station when you went to identify the body?" She had been so preoccupied with her own problems she'd forgotten about Nana.

"We never made it there. Dylan insisted that we come back for you."

Dylan reclined in his seat, his voice calmer now. "When I thought about the situation, I decided it was too risky to leave you alone for any length of time, and your dad agreed."

For the first time Jay acknowledged Dylan's help. "Whatever the reason, I'm just glad you showed up when you did."

"Jay." Chrissie gasped as she turned to him. "Are you paying Dylan a compliment?"

Without hesitation, he retorted. "No."

"Sorry I asked." Turning to William, she inquired, "What are we going to do about Nana?"

William glared straight ahead and mused, speaking more to himself than to anyone else in the car. "It's evident to me that someone is trying to use your grandmother to lure you into a trap." He fixed his gaze on the windshield, and remained silent for several seconds.

Chrissie tapped her finger against the dashboard. "We can't sit around and do nothing. We need to find out what happened to Nana."

Dylan placed his hand on her shoulder once again. "We will, but we need to make sure you're safe before we resume the search."

Leaning forward, Jayden concurred. "He's right, Chrissie. Whoever has your grandmother is using her to get to you. We can't take the chance that they will get you, too." Chrissie was amazed. For the second time, he agreed with Dylan.

"I'll take her to Carthexia like I planned. She'll be safe there. We can leave as soon as she gets a few personals items. They'll take care of her needs when she arrives."

William nodded. "That sounds like a good plan."

It was Jayden's job to protect Chrissie during vulnerable times, and he took the task seriously. "I don't really like the idea of having her so far away. No one there knows her."

Chrissie straightened her back. Looking over her shoulder, she said, "Stop talking about me as if I'm not here. I'm not going anywhere." Her mind wondered briefly. *"I refuse to allow three men to make decisions for me."*

"What are you talking about?" Dylan retorted. "You were looking forward to going earlier. What happened?"

"That was before I realized my grandmother is bait. I'm not going into hiding when someone is using her to get to me. Besides. I want to finish this term. The semester will end in a month."

From the backseat, Dylan barked his orders. "You're going, Christina."

She placed one hand atop the other and cut her eyes at him. "No. I'm not. And you can't make me. You don't get to make decisions for me."

"Actually, I can make you."

"We'll see." She turned to face the windshield. William never commented on their squabble. From the smirk on his face, it was easy to tell his money was on Chrissie.

~THE END OF VOLUME TWO~

.

About the Author

Payton A. Whitfield

TRANSCENDING DAWN~VAMPIRE SERIES

My favorite authors are Edgar Allan Poe and Stephen King. Both of whom have a flare for the macabre. Growing up, nothing got my blood pumping like a tale that sent chills down my spine. As I matured, I also enjoyed reading a good love story, so I decided to merge the two genres. Writing thrillers allows me to escape from the daily grind and sends my senses on adventures of my own ghoulish creation.

Recently, I pursued my dream and signed on with Topaz Publishing. There, I will produce a series of vampire tales entitled Transcending Dawn. Christina, a vampire, is the heroine in these stories, and Dylan, a drachmon is the hero. Volume One introduces this unlikely couple. Then it's on to high adventure, romance, action, and intrigue. Each volume brings the reader closer to learning the truth about this spirited pair.

Each month, Topaz Publishing will release one of my wonderful tales, just perfect for those who love vampires and creatures of the night.

http://www.topazpublishingllc.com.

My website is www.pawhitfield.webs.com.